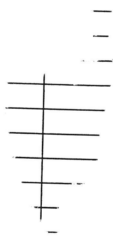

Pillion Riders

Pillion Riders

Elisabeth Russell Taylor

with an Introduction by Peter Vansittart

W F HOWES LTD

This large print edition published in 2006 by
W F Howes Ltd
Unit 4, Rearsby Business Park, Gaddesby Lane,
Rearsby, Leicester LE7 4YH

1 3 5 7 9 10 8 6 4 2

First published in the United Kingdom in 1993
by Peter Owen Publishers

A CIP catalogue record for this book is available
from the British Library

ISBN 1 84632 430 0

Typeset by Palimpsest Book Production Limited,
Polmont, Stirlingshire
Printed and bound in Great Britain
by Antony Rowe Ltd, Chippenham, Wilts.

CONTENTS

INTRODUCTION

Elisabeth Russell Taylor is acclaimed by Shena Mackay, A.S. Byatt, Elaine Feinstein, D.J. Taylor and Andrew Sinclair – a formidable posse contemptuous of fashionable but indiscriminate hyperbole. Her work, like her personality, is decisive and sharp-edged, emerging not only from sophisticated taste but from a varied strata of livelihoods. She has been a university lecturer, broadcaster, journalist; has kept an antiques stall, assisted a movie star, survived an artists' commune, mingled with international painters, composers, writers; is an authority on plants, specialised cookery and, notably, on Proust.

Varied experience, not guaranteed to display people at their best, has allowed Taylor ample opportunities to observe their quirks, diversity, inconsistencies, lack of scruple. Her people are never stereotypes but always individually drawn. Like Sybille Bedford, Taylor knows the imaginative possibilities provided by gaps between slabs of information, the dangers of knowing and revealing too much; thus the reader becomes an active collaborator rather than a passive sponge. Taylor assumes readers are not only physically mature but mentally adult.

Her writing for children and for films has perhaps sharpened her flair for cutting the superfluous while enlarging small but telling details: a woman shaving, a rich child's rudeness to a shop assistant. And though adroit with stories, she is more rewarding with the novel, more ambitious, allowing for the development of character, the long comedy of mixed motives, unconscious conflicts, casual mis-understandings and complex first causes. This is emphatic in *Pillion Riders*, itself originating in a short story. In Taylor's novels, people are touched – if often reluctantly or unwittingly – by the wider worlds of politics, hatreds, poverty, the pressures of a past made monstrous by preventable ignorance, prejudice, injustice, war and Holocaust, in which propagandists can smoothly publicise Auschwitz as a 'sanatorium' and blur murder into 'liquidation' or 'resettlement'. The novels unfold secret his-tories lurking behind sensational headlines, those of muffled betrayals, thoughtless irresponsibility, stupid and merciless adults. Overwhelming evils can enlarge from hushed corridors, small rooms, a petty quarrel. History, Marx once wrote, is made behind people's backs. One doubts whether Elisabeth Russell Taylor would applaud T.S. Eliot's assertion that, paradoxically, it is better to do evil than to do nothing – evil activities proving that at least we exist.

★   ★   ★

Many excellent writers reassert a popular view of life, thus flattering, reassuring and delighting readers. But Taylor is not renowned for flattery: she queries, contradicts or ridicules official truths and accepted opinions, and levies an international perspective on minds incorrigibly insular, while adding her own distinctive vision. 'Vision' is admittedly, like 'sublime' and 'fantastic', too often applied to something silly, though not here. Taylor's vision, though serious, at times fierce, is tempered by humour. Not that of rollicking, stand-up comics, but sly, oblique, even throwaway, akin to that of E.M. Forster, Muriel Spark, indeed Jane Austen. Seldom markedly genial, it has the effrontery of original perception. Her style is crisp and economical, her themes sometimes alarmingly perceptive. She crafts both the odd and the familiar with sufficient small shocks to engross the most hungry reader of commercial fiction.

A graphic sense of place is evident in the novels, taking the characters from Poland (*Swann Song*) to Denmark (*Tomorrow*), Switzerland (*I is Another*) and France (*Pillion Riders*). Taylor has literally explored locations associated with favourite writers: the Wordsworths, Clare, Proust, Alain-Fournier.

> We had returned to the land without a name – the lost paradise of childhood. It was not merely a state of mind, it was a real location in the heart of France. This is where Jean-Claude belonged: on the desolate

sandy heaths that break against distant shores of pines; by pools of still water fringed with reeds and willows; on stony paths ground by wagon wheels. His whole and deepest self was so drenched in the brooding melancholy of Solange as to make his years in Paris unreal.

An echo of Vigny's 'God! How sad is the sound of a horn heard deep in the woods.' Flaubert interpreted his novels as colours: *Salammbô* – purple, *Madame Bovary* – mouldy wood-louse grey. Taylor's books might be seen as twilit violet, punctuated by dark streaks nuanced between charnel black and autumnal browns. Colours illuminate her pages: in tints of summer sky, gardens, a hushed wood, fruit glowing in a market.

Pillion Riders enlarges a favourite theme: the challenge of frustration, with surrender or partial triumph. Opal, young and culturally, socially, sexually inexperienced, has been married off by an uncaring father to Helmut, older, rich, decent but unimaginative – a Forsyte incapable of passion. Becalmed in luxuriant idleness, style without substance, Opal is taken to Paris by Helmut, who is anxious to introduce her to the conventional museums, fashionable galleries and restaurants, modish opinions. Paris indeed transforms her taste and personality, though in a manner that can only outrage Helmut. Her deeper instincts are excited by another Paris, first glimpsed from a motorcycle pillion while clasping a stranger's back. A Paris of squalid dwellings, vivid streets, grim doss-houses, all mysterious, beguiling, perhaps perilous, certainly sensual and removed from smart chatter and tourism. Opal elopes with the young and exciting Jean-Claude, a composer and free spirit – all that Helmut is not. Jean-Claude is gifted, combative, supercilious; also a self-righteous, arrogant, anti-Semitic thief who embodies the belief, more wide-spread than it should be, that the exceptional artist is entitled to exceptional licence and can ignore, without question, kindness, honest companionship, sexual equality, common decency. Living with him, Opal unwillingly recognises that despite Jean-Claude's enchantments, she has exchanged one form of slavery for another. And yet:

> It did not enter my head that I might have the seeds of a talent, that I too might have a career and that I should be preparing myself for it. Father had told me repeatedly that as a woman, my role was to surrender to a man: that submission and compliance would be the meaning of my life . . . I had not found meaning with Helmut. I had with Jean-Claude.

To add much more would spoil the outcome. When Jean-Claude is commissioned to write an opera based on Alain-Fournier's classic novel, *Le*

Grand Meaulnes, Pillion Riders is elevated to a further dimension, from plot to a form of poetry that should delight readers responsive to that small masterpiece of adolescent yearnings, the lure of distance, spells of ancient landscapes, woods, lost domains: of the oblique, half-seen, the imagined. Epithets like 'poetic', 'haunting', 'elegiac' easily degenerate to exclamatory gush, but are surely appropriate here.

Peter Vansittart
London 2005

LONDON

In nature there is a species of parasite for almost every species of everything else.

I was a very old woman before I found myself reviewing the past. I do not know why I had avoided it so long, whether out of too little interest or too great a fear, but I do believe I would have allowed the events of my youth, events that were of the utmost importance at the time, to have lain in my absence of memory until I died had it not been for the unexpected visit of a friend I had not seen or heard from for forty years.

'You are still very lovely!' Geza said, and I was reminded of his gallantry. 'How is it that you live alone?' he asked. 'Tell me,' he went on, 'what was it that made you leave Jean-Claude?'

Jean-Claude! The name so hit me that it shook me. I shivered. 'Pass me that little rug by your side. I'll have it round my shoulders.' Geza rose and gently laid the rug about me, pressing my shoulders with his hands as a token of intimacy.

I am nineteen. I have been married off to Helmut Gressinger, a business associate of my father, some- one he has known all my life. I know I have been 'married off'. It was Father who brought Helmut to the house and introduced him to me, it was his suggestion that I consider Helmut as a possible husband, and he took pains to convince me of the suitability of Helmut's proposal.

'We have to bear in mind your condition, child. It would not be fair for you to lead some un-suspecting youth into matrimony. He would expect children, an heir, and with your condition . . . No! It is out of the question. Helmut is fond of you. He was fond of your mother. He is an ideal match.'

I see Father's point. Helmut is a kind man, and responsible – but I cannot fall in love with him for that. I try, but all I manage is a feeling of gratitude towards a man who does not mock my too narrow hips and too flat chest, and never calls me 'laddie' as others have. He takes me to live in London in a house with eight bedrooms, four bathrooms, a drawing-room, dining-room, study and billiards-room. And servants' quarters. The house stands in a private road overlooking Hyde Park. The running of the house is left in the capable hands of Mrs Page, the chauffeur's wife. Helmut says I am to leave everything to Mrs Page, but that if I so wish I may order and arrange the flowers and decide on the menus for dinner. And if Mrs Page is in agree-ment I may attend to other small matters that might contribute to the personality of the house.

Helmut has business associates to dinner at least twice a week. We are invited out at least twice a

4

week. Helmut likes the theatre and the opera, and explains that I must appear in the latest fashions. His friend Olga who, he says, conveys a stylishness he appreciates, will take me to the right places to buy my clothes and have my hair set. I do not dare confess to Helmut that Olga makes me nervous. I have never come across this type of person before. Where I was brought up, in the provinces, people were not smart. Olga is too smart for words. I cannot imagine her ever dirty or ruffled. She has blood-red finger-nails an inch long. I bet they could scratch.

I take breakfast in bed. This is something new to me and I do not altogether enjoy it. It is hard for me to lie listening to the sound of the vacuum cleaner, smelling kidneys and bacon being prepared for Helmut. I do not rise and take my bath until Helmut has left for the office. He established this routine for me. He says this way he can keep his last glimpse of me against the pink silk sheets. He telephones mid-morning to ask how I am and what plans I have for the day. I find it difficult to talk at any length. I have no plans. All the things I am good at he has servants to do. Not wishing to disappoint him, I make up something. I do not tell him that I shall probably sit and talk all day to the housemaid.

'Rest, my love, my little night-owl!' Because he has time for me only in the evenings and at weekends, he likes me to be fresh and wide awake for him then. He needs only three hours sleep a night, which surprises me. 'As you get older . . .' He reminds me that as one ages one needs less sleep.

We have been married two years. Helmut has had to be away increasingly on business. Sometimes, during his absences, Olga takes me to a matinee theatre performance or an exhibition. She says I need to have my outlook broadened. One afternoon she takes me to Dr Friedman, Helmut's doctor. He prescribes vitamin pills and a tonic. He asks me how much exercise I take. He is shocked by how little it is. He tells me I must walk an hour a day. Since I live by the park, that should be quite pleasant for me. But it seems he wrote something rather different to Helmut. 'Your wife is unwell. She is melancholic! Take her away, somewhere beautiful where she can feast her senses.'

Helmut's first thought is of Venice. His second, Paris. He settles on Paris because a friend from his student days in Heidelberg works at Unesco.

'A most fascinating man. You'll love him. He'll remind me of everything I should show you.'

'This hotel was built by Mansard for Armand-Louis de Gontaut-Biron, duc de Lauzun . . .' Helmut sounds like a museum guide as he walks me along the corridors of the Ritz Hotel, corridors lined with show-cases filled with priceless jewellery and small works of art, leading me into the dining-room for dinner. 'Proust used to dine here. I shall get the waiter to point out his table. He used the Ritz as his grocer's. He used to send his chauffeur here for a bottle of iced beer in the middle of the night if he was thirsty.' I do not like to admit to Helmut that I do not know who Mr Proust is. Nor do I tell him that, to my way of thinking, whoever he was, he was disgracefully inconsiderate to disturb his chauffeur's sleep over such a trifling requirement. And if he was rich enough to employ a chauffeur, did he not own a refrigerator?

It is the first morning of my first visit to Paris. We have breakfasted on *croissants* and *brioches* – my first – and the most delicious *café au lait*. My dear husband is beaming with delight as he leads me across the Place Vendôme towards Schiaparelli. 'I've always wanted to see you in bright, geranium-pink silk,' he murmurs, as much to himself as to me. He is gazing into the shop window. Admiring.

I beg him not to insist. 'Please let me wear what I feel most comfortable in.'

He does not insist, although I know he tires of my favourite black. A uniformed doorman, looking every inch a general, holds open the heavy plate-glass door and we pass through into warm, scented air which smells expensive. Helmut buys me a flask of scent called 'Shocking'.

In the Tuileries, smartly dressed little children huddle in groups on the gravel paths, close to their nannies, who are gossiping on ornate park benches. I do not speak or understand more than a few words of French, and it seems to me as we pass the nannies and their charges that they are arguing, that they are in uproar, that soon there will be trouble. I ask Helmut what is wrong.

He laughs. 'There is nothing amiss, my dear. The French are excitable people, they are easily roused. That's all.' And he fastens his arm more tightly around my own.

Notre-Dame is easily the largest, most awe-inspiring cathedral I have ever seen. As I stand looking up at the right portico, making out the scenes from the life of Saint Anne, I feel dizzy with intoxication. While Helmut sits on the terrace of the Café de la Place reading *Le Monde*, I explore the sullen cool of Notre-Dame. Whereas every-thing is so noisily animated in the streets of Paris, gloom encases the stone of the cathedral and I feel deeply at peace. I vaguely recall something of our local church, St Stephen's, and Mother and Father on Sunday mornings.

When I rejoin Helmut I rather hope he is going to suggest luncheon, followed by a rest at the hotel. He does no such thing. He takes me to a *brasserie* in the Place St Michel for oysters and then announces enthusiastically he is going to introduce me to some of the masterpieces in the Louvre.

'You will assuredly want to see the *Mona Lisa*, Veronese's *Les Noces de Cana*, Caravaggio's *Death of the Virgin* . . .' I do so wish Helmut had not suggested the Louvre. I have heard tell of its long corridors and ill-lit galleries. I do not want to see the *Mona Lisa* or any other of the paintings Helmut imagines I want to see. I cannot see the point of gaping at pictures and being obliged to like master-pieces, as they are called. Olga has taken me to the National Gallery in London on several occa-sions to look at medieval paintings, because she knows I love the Holy Family. But once I have seen a couple of Crucifixions, Depositions and Last Suppers, I feel quite ill. It is all so tragic. And I certainly cannot see the point of other pictures, those that do not tell an important story. If I could have just one picture on my wall at home I might come to love it, but I never remember any details of things I see in museums and galleries. You cannot put a finger between all the paintings on Helmut's walls. I ask Helmut whether he does not think it rather rude to look at a picture in ten seconds, then turn away and look at another. 'The artist may have spent years and years painting that!' I point out to him.

He laughs. 'You are adorable!' he says. He is standing in front of overdressed men and women in a garden that looks to me like a well-kept field. The women are seated on swings, the men are lolling on the grass, eating from picnic hampers. Little black boys are pouring wine. I feel the same way I feel when I have inadvisably consumed a box of Turkish delight at one sitting. But Helmut loves these scenes, particularly.

'One of Watteau's favourite places was the

9

Luxembourg Garden. I shall take you there!'

And he does: to see the Medici Fountain, whose waters fall into a rectangular basin designed to make it seem that they are flowing uphill. I quite like that. But I cannot respond to the sculptures. All those people frozen in the most unlikely positions . . . Anyhow, I find these formal surroundings enclose despondency.

'Isn't there somewhere else we might go?'

'Of course, my dearest.' And Helmut ushers me down a side-street into the hushed seriousness of a *salon de thé*.

I am twig-thin and may snap. I am exhausted. We are leaning on the Pont au Double watching the Seine as it flows through the hoops formed by the bridges. Helmut wants me to admire the reflection of their arches in the ruffled, pewter-dull water. 'We shall take a *bateau-mouche* – but not today.'

I am relieved that this jaunt is postponed. Throughout the day Helmut has spoken little. In the taxi on our way back to the Ritz he explains that there is only one subject he likes to think about on a journey, whether it is through a foreign country or merely through a city, and that is what he will be having for dinner that night. Then he embarks on a description of all the great chefs of France and their wonderful inventions. 'There is nothing they cannot transform into peerless dishes!' And he waits for me to tell him which I might prefer: lobster claws, pigs' feet, bulls' testicles . . . I feel sick.

While I am taking a nap Helmut goes down to the bar to meet a business friend. He returns to our suite in time to change and suggest what I should wear. When I am dressed and made up he makes me close my eyes while he fastens something round my neck. 'You may open them now!'

I see an exquisite choker of pearls fastened at the front, with four large opals.

'It's beautiful! Thank you so very much.'

Helmut does not like to be thanked, whether for a present or an occasion. He dismisses my gratitude with a gesture. He brushes his right hand through the air as if he were ridding himself of a midge. He prefers to tell me something about Otto von Kramitz, his friend, who heads a section at Unesco concerned with Central Africa. Otto is the same age as Helmut, fifty-eight, and unmarried. Like Helmut he had the good sense – and good fortune – to leave Germany in 1933. He has since amassed a fine collection of African art, including a Nok head from northern Nigeria, 'rice gods' from Sierra Leone and crocodile-teeth charms from Madagascar. Otto and he were inseparable as students, and since then have made every effort to get together whenever they find themselves within a few hours' travelling distance of one another. I am struck by how excited Helmut is at the prospect of seeing his old friend. He does not normally expose his feelings for anyone but me.

An attendant leads us from the foyer of the building to the door of Mr von Kramitz's office.

He had been adamant about not letting us make our own way. He opens the office door and announces us before turning on his heel. The office is vast, at least forty feet long. I do not imagine Mr von Kramitz heard us announced, but he notices the light from the open door. He rises from his seat at the far side of his desk and walks towards us with his arms outstretched, as if to gather both Helmut and me in a single embrace. I stand a little to one side, and notice another man seated at the near side of the desk. He has his back to us. While Otto and Helmut exchange salutations in German, I find my attention transfixed by the immobile stranger. He is dressed in a khaki military-style rain-jacket and heavy brown leather boots. He has a mop of fair hair. I believe he must be young. I wonder why he does not rise to greet us and why Otto does not introduce him. Why has he not removed his street clothes? Has he just arrived? Absently, I shake Otto's extended hand, but I am not concentrating on the exchange. I am consumed by a weird but powerful certainty that whereas Otto von Kramitz – elegantly suited, bathed in eau de Portugal, exquisitely mannered – will play no part in my affections, this younger man will play a crucial role.

Otto has both my hands in his. He is telling me that he has heard much about me, that he has looked forward to meeting me since he read the announcement of our marriage in *The Times*, quite by chance. Had he not been in Sierra Leone he would of course have been at the wedding. He hopes I liked the Yoruba diving-board he sent Helmut. 'I would have preferred to have delivered it personally, of course. I would have expected to be best man!' he adds and, turning from me, he thumps Helmut affectionately on the back. He is so sorry, he says, that I have been unwell. He hopes that it was nothing serious and is sure a visit to the city of love will have me thoroughly restored. Throughout his warm, enthusiastic display the young man remains seated, his back to me.

'I have reserved a table at La Boîte,' Otto announces.

'Oh, surely not. Why not somewhere more traditional?' My husband is clearly disappointed.

'La Boîte is all the rage this season. Your beautiful young wife will see *le tout Paris*.'

I can never remember how it came about that, instead of accompanying Helmut and Otto in the official Mercedes, I rode to La Boîte on the back of Jean-Claude's motor cycle. I do not even remember how we were introduced – for we must have been – or anything of the discussion that surely arose when I chose to travel with Jean-Claude rather than my husband. I can only recall – and this vividly – how, wearing my tight-skirted black velvet suit, my new pearl choker and the little half-veil that was so fashionable that year, I rode across Paris with my arms clasped tight round a man to whom I had not spoken and had not closely

13

observed, yet to whom I felt inextricably bound. When he helped me off the pillion at the entrance to La Boîte, we stood face to face for a few seconds. We stared at one another. He said something in French. I said something in English. I discovered he had as few words of English at his disposal as I had of French.

But I remember well how shocked I was by the irritable tone in which Otto addressed Jean-Claude and me when we entered the restaurant. Helmut and Otto were seated at a table when we came in.

'Sit here!' Otto roared at Jean-Claude in English, pointing to the chair next to his own. 'Sit there, with your husband,' he ordered me pointedly, indicating the banquette against the wall. 'You have to face into the restaurant so that you can watch *le tout Paris*.'

My husband ignores the tension. As I drop into the seat beside him, he kisses my cheek and takes the starched white damask napkin, which is floating like a boat at sea on my deep cobalt plate, shakes it out and spreads it across my lap. Leaning towards me, he whispers 'That's T.S. Eliot', and nods his head in the direction of a plain, middle-aged man who reminds me of Mr Savage, Father's bank manager, who used to come in for a drink on Christmas Eve. I do not get the chance to ask who Mr Eliot is. Otto, my husband and Jean-Claude suddenly have a great many things to talk about very quickly in French. I am left to my own

14

thoughts, which do not adequately detain me, so, because I am rather bored, I strain my ears to hear what plain Mr Eliot is saying to his equally plain companion.

'Neither of the protagonists is invested with much humanity, either for good or evil,' he is remarking to his friend. I think he must be trying out a speech. People do not 'talk' to one another like that. And later he asks his friend if she would like 'a fruit'. I think he should have offered her 'some fruit' or just 'fruit'. But I quite forget to check this with Helmut later.

'And how is your partridge?' There is a lull in the conversation and my husband turns to me. He is always anxious that I should enjoy the items on the menu that he selects for me.

'Very nice,' I reassure him.

'They are the celebrated *perdrix aux truffes*,' he explains. 'I do hope you are going to please me by rounding off your meal with the *granité de melon au champagne*.' But I hardly listen. Whatever my preference, I know that to please Helmut I shall let him decide for me. And just at that very minute I notice that Yves Montand is being shown to a table across from ours, and Juliette Greco is talking to the *maître d'hôtel*. I am so excited. 'Look! Look!' I point.

'Ssh!' my husband hisses. 'You're behaving like a child.'

I feel humiliated, but I know he is right. I only hope that Jean-Claude has not noticed my *faux pas*.

But if he has not understood the exchange, Jean-Claude has registered the tone in which it was conveyed. He pats my knee lightly under the table. I put my hand surreptitiously under the starched folds of the table-cloth and for a split second we touch fingertips. When I look up into his face we exchange understanding.

I cannot help wondering about Otto's behaviour towards Jean-Claude: it is strange. He keeps touching the young man's arm, resting his own arm around the back of his chair, and when Jean-Claude says something that amuses him he strokes his cheek.

We have finished eating and are drinking coffee when my husband and Otto start to discuss what will be the most interesting and amusing things for me to do and see in Paris.

'But Opal must decide for herself,' Otto says, smiling indulgently. 'She's not a child.'

I am surprised to find myself saying that what I should most like would be to see Paris by night from the back of Jean-Claude's motor cycle.

'*Ne sois pas trop tard!*' Otto orders Jean-Claude as we emerge into the rue Jacob.

'No,' my husband adds, 'I don't want Opal getting over-tired.'

It is a balmy evening in early September. Jean-Claude rides slowly over one bridge and back across another. We stop to watch the embankment lights drip into the water and tremble there. Accelerating, he rides me round and round the Place de la

16

Concorde. I notice how the light is yellow from the illuminated fountains, and his headlights ablaze make the sooty leaves of the plane trees appear more glorious than they are. Then he stops for me to see what looks like a stationary herd of black beetles as far as the Arc de Triomphe. I keep on thinking: This is me. I am being shown Paris. I pinch myself.

Because I did not know Paris at the time, I do not now remember the landmarks Jean-Claude pointed out to me or the route we took to Montmartre. But I do remember the effect of the spellbinding view from la Butte. It was far in excess of anything I could have imagined, anything that picture-postcard images had suggested. I believe my excitement was tinged with apprehension. I think I knew that the view would not have inspired in me quite the same nervous exultation had I been seeing it for the first time with Helmut.

Jean-Claude does not take me back to the Ritz as he said he would. He takes me to his attic on the outskirts of Paris, in a *quartier* called Reine les Falaises.

It seems a long, long way from the city. Eventually, we dismount in the tree-lined rue Victorie. Jean-Claude pushes his motor cycle through the small iron gate provided for those on foot, beside the huge iron gates for cars. I find we are in a broad courtyard. Jean-Claude props his motor cycle against the wall of a bleak, stuccoed house. The lights from the street shine brighter than those in

London streets and I can make out the size and shape of a four-storey building, beside which a path leads to a *pavillon*. The front door to the house is open. Jean-Claude takes my hand and leads me into the darkness. He turns a switch that dimly lights the stairs and leads me quietly to the top of the house. The lights unnervingly extinguish themselves well before we reach the attic. I am glad of Jean-Claude's hand. I am still feeling a mixture of excitement and fear.

It must be late. While Jean-Claude takes a key to unlock the attic door, I feel a sharp stab behind my ribs. My heart is thumping. I think my knees may give way. Now Jean-Claude has his arm round me and is drawing me into the room and settling me in a chair. He is throwing off his coat and feeding logs into the stove. I can make out three areas in the attic. One must be for sleeping: I see the bed. The one we are in is for working, perhaps; there is a table and a chair under the window. The third must be for the preparation of food. I see a sink and notice it is served by a single tap. There is evidently no bathroom.

I feel embarrassed. How can I explain? I get up from the chair and wander to the door leading to the stairs. Jean-Claude understands and points down the stairwell. He presses the button for the *minuterie*, the time-switch for the light, and I go back down. There is just one WC for the house. It is no more than a hole in the ground, lighted from the stairs by a gap in the door. First, I am mystified as to how to negotiate it, then I am repelled. The light on the stairs has extinguished itself. In the eerie unfamiliarity of my surroundings I wonder what on earth I am doing here.

Jean-Claude has boiled a kettle and poured hot water into a bowl. He leaves me behind a screen as he tidies things away out of sight. I reflect that there is no chaos here, only untidiness. For chaos there would need to be more things. He takes a clean shirt out of a cupboard and hands it to me round the screen, so as not to embarrass me.

Over a glass of wine in a bar in Montmartre, Jean-Claude and I, with our half-dozen words, had made known to one another our desire. We probably communicated something rather different, rather less subtle, than we would have done if we had shared a language. Whatever it was that drew us together that night was new to me, and unexpected. It was also urgent, and seemed profound. It was not altogether sexual, and yet the only expression we could give it was sexual. Each of us experienced agony at the thought of losing the other. We were one another's life-raft. And since we were almost wordless, the only way we had to reassure one another was to make love again and again.

With great gentleness, Jean-Claude removes the shirt with which he has provided me. '*Que tu es belle, ma pauvre fille*,' he murmurs. I understand 'belle' but am I right in thinking that 'pauvre' means poor? Whatever else, I am actually quite rich – or my husband is . . .

I have never been with a young man. I have known only my husband. The comparison is odious and makes me feel uncomfortable. Helmut's body is hairy as an ape's, and his stomach swells indecently. He is not demanding, I have to say. Once a week he covers my body with the weight of his own and ejaculates quickly. Had I known the words at the time I would have thought *Ça vous donne tant de plaisir et moi si peu de peine.* Jean-Claude is slim and his skin silky. He smells of hay. He finds ways of pleasing me that I have never so much as imagined, let alone experienced. But I am puzzled why it is he weeps, and why, in response to his tears, I too weep. Neither of us sleeps that night. Sleep would be a waste of time. All the while we make love we speak uncomprehendingly to one another, but we understand something beyond words.

Between making love and resting to regain the strength to make love again, Jean-Claude gets out of bed, puts logs in the stove and laboriously grinds coffee-beans. There is something in this ritual that impresses me. The full implications of it will reveal themselves only months later. We sit side by side, naked on the bed, drinking our coffee and smoking Gauloises. We try out sign language to amplify what we can find words to say. What is obvious to both of us is that we are enjoying one another.

I have no idea where in relation to the city Reine

lies. It seems distant. It is utterly quiet. As we lie together, resting, my face on his chest, his arm about me, all we hear is the hooting of an owl. And so it comes as a rude shock when peace is shattered at about 4.30 a.m. by the sound of a lorry driving down the lane into the courtyard, where it revs its engine while the two huge iron gates to the street are being dragged over the cobbles.

'Maman, Papa,' Jean-Claude explains. I do not have the vocabulary to inquire what they are about at that hour.

I am aware that Jean-Claude's feelings towards me are protective ones. He appears to feel a sort of pity for me. I am puzzled about this. His life is evidently much harder than mine. I do not live in a cold-water flat, sharing a single hole in the ground with all the tenants in my house. I do not carpet my rooms with newspaper and curtain my window with sacking . . . But his gestures are maternal. He folds me in his arms, gently securing my head between his face and shoulder, and rocks me to and fro, as if I were a child.

And I feel I belong in that attic with him.

It is some time after his parents' lorry disturbs us and drives away that Jean-Claude takes a framed photograph down from the wall and puts it in my hands. I see it is a hand-tinted likeness of a lovely young woman closely resembling himself.

'Sister,' he manages, 'Dead!' he adds, passing

his hand horizontally across his neck and making an unmistakable sound: the awesome truth. The rest he mimes. He discovered her. He cut her down. But too late. And he was devastated. He holds out his wrists and I can just make out the hair-thin bleached scars. And when he sees that I have understood, he raises his chin and moans to the heavens as a tethered dog wails to the moon.

I take him in my arms and rock him as he rocked me. Once composed, he disengages himself and kneels by the side of the bed. He takes my left hand in his and draws off my wedding-ring. Solemnly he replaces it, but on the fourth finger of my right hand. 'French' he explains. I understand: he is now my French husband. He murmurs my name and I answer with his. 'Man and woman!' he manages triumphantly. And then he draws me out of bed, drapes me in a rug and sits me at his table. First, he empties the contents of his pockets and places a bunch of keys, a packet of cigarettes and a lighter, and a few francs, before me. Next he throws open the door of the cupboard and points. I make out two shirts, a pair of trousers, a couple of sweaters, a pair of boots and a small pile of what looks to be odd socks. He watches my face closely as I take in the contents, registering as little surprise as I am able. Next, bending over me, he opens the drawer in his table half-way and takes out a handful of notebooks, showing me the stave lines, two bottles of ink and some pencils and pens. Then he draws me into the kitchen area and points to the shelves above the porcelain sink. I can see packets of noodles, salt and butter. He throws his arms wide, indicating that he has shown me all his belongings, everything. Looking into my face, which he holds with one finger under my chin, he whispers: 'C'*est tout*!'. I understand. These are his worldly goods. He is inviting me to share them. Or is he?

I was confused. I did not understand what it was Jean-Claude expected of me. Nor did I recognize my own feelings and what they might lead me to do. I tried to compose myself, to identify them. I was filled with longing for something Jean-Claude might have to offer me but to which I felt in no way entitled. I thought back to my entitlement, and my blood ran cold. Now, all these years later, I see that, unconsciously, I knew I could never unknow what I had experienced that night, and that all else would compare inadequately. I do remember wondering how I was going to continue in my marriage.

I look at my watch. I wash and dress at speed. All the while my thoughts run ahead: his sister is dead, he is deeply distressed. Otto von Kramitz likes him a lot. He is very poor, perhaps Otto helps him . . . He composes music, but earns money for his scant needs as a messenger-boy. This is his home. What a pity he speaks only French. He is young, youthful in a way some men never are . . . Helmut, for example. He is beautiful. He makes love as if my pleasure were as important to him as his own. And when I am fully dressed, in clothes that in the light of morning look hopelessly unsuited to their surroundings, I walk round the attic and peer out of the window, beyond the iron gates, into the road. I am determined to memorize every detail of the room. The books beside the bed: one from the Série Noire, *Vilain*. The brand of coffee-beans in the shiny, walnut packet: Mokarex. And, I shall remember, across the road, on the blue-washed wall of the *épicerie*, the white letters that spell out tantalizingly (for I did not understand their meaning) *Exigez le slip Rasurel*.

I do not allow Jean-Claude to drive me back to the Ritz. I want my last glimpse of him to be in his *quartier*. And I would be embarrassed to alight from the pillion of his motor cycle at the feet of the head porter. Instead, I let him walk me to the Place Victorie and hail me a taxi. I do not remember whether we embraced. I do not remember how we parted. I do remember that once in the taxi I was overwhelmed, flooded by a sense of utter dejection: the physical pain of loss.

Helmut is seated in his Sulka dressing-gown, tucking into breakfast in the sitting-room of our suite. I have to knock several times before he hears me and opens the door. I imagine I knocked quietly;

I was paralysed with cold fear. But I was not only embarrassed, I was irritated. I did not want to be there. I did not know what to say. 'I hope you weren't anxious,' is what I do say.

'Dear child, not in the least. Otto assured me that Jean-Claude is an expert cyclist. Come now, have something to eat.'

'But were you not – I don't quite know how to put it – a bit annoyed that I didn't return? Didn't you mind my spending the night with a young man?'

'Not when the young man in question was Jean-Claude, dearest. I know what the situation is between him and Otto. Otto minded!' Helmut roars with laughter, mirthlessly. 'Poor Otto, we sat in the bar together until the early hours . . . He tells me that so far as women are concerned, Jean-Claude will always remain faithful to the memory of his sister. She is the only woman he ever loved.'

I turn away. I understand less than I did. Least of all, my confusion. I am determined, however, that my husband shall not observe this, or my tears.

'And now, dearest, once you have had something to eat, do go and bathe and change into something less formal. We are going first to the Eiffel Tower. We shall take luncheon at the summit. And this afternoon we shall walk in the Palais-Royal Garden and visit one or two antique shops.' He inquires rather vaguely whether I have any shopping I want to do, but does not seem to notice that I do not answer. He is exceptionally happy.

25

I recall this because I felt more miserable than I could remember ever having felt, and it seemed strange to me that a husband and wife could feel so much at variance.

As we emerge from the hotel into the Place Vendôme, Helmut points to a poster advertising the *Folies Bergère*. 'That's where we shall be going tonight, little one.' He puts his arm round my shoulder. 'Dearest Opal, you'll love it, it's so glamorous. Every day we are together I learn a little more about what pleases you. I have a lovely surprise for you . . .' Does this mean Jean-Claude will be joining us? My heart leaps. 'When we get back to London I shall arrange the delivery of a motor cycle. Page will take you out and about on it when I don't need him with the car.'

I pass the following days in something of a daze, constantly on the alert for the sight of Jean-Claude. Every time I hear a motor cycle rev up, tyres skid to a halt or a klaxon sound, I look about me. Helmut and Otto have drawn up an itinerary of the sites I should visit. Helmut races me from the remains of Roman Paris at the Arènes de Lutèce to the remains of medieval Paris at the church of St Pierre and the Cluny Museum. He is especially keen for me to see a selection of the best art nouveau buildings, he says. I hate them. Particularly one *appartement* block decorated all over with ceramic thistles. Surely, I say to Helmut, only a donkey would want to browse in a place with thistles all over the doors and windows and paths? He does not agree, and takes me to the building he likes best of all, with concrete eau-de-Nil seahorses let into the walls. I cannot take this seriously. It is a joke to me. I tell Helmut that I do not think it reasonable to fashion a joke that will last hundreds of years. But he does not regard this decoration as a joke in poor taste. Nor does he feel any need to discuss what he sees with me. He does not need my opinion to help him form his own: he has decided on *everything*. Ages ago. At each site he hands me the guidebook, turns to the relevant page and recommends that I read in detail what I am about to see. I hate this method of sightseeing. On the other hand, I am relieved to be able to conceal from my husband my complete lack of knowledge about everything – dates, architectural styles, movements in painting. I keep thinking that what I should really like to be doing, in this glorious autumn weather, is sitting on the banks of the Seine watching the boats go by. With Jean-Claude.

One evening, when Helmut can see I am more than usually tired and quiet, he suggests I take dinner in our suite and retire early. He will attend the opera with Otto. I am careful not to show how overjoyed I am.

'I am tired,' I agree. 'If I don't get some rest, I may not be able to keep up with our hectic sightseeing tomorrow.'

I feel rather refreshed after I have eaten a light supper and drunk half a bottle of champagne. It is good to be alone with my thoughts of Jean-Claude. What, I wonder, is he doing and with whom? I realize I do not even know his surname. If I knew his surname I could telephone him – but he is not on the telephone . . . At the time I did not know of the existence of the miraculous *bleu*, the *pneumatique*. If I had, I believe I would have sent him a message. I want to see him more than anything in the world. What would happen if I simply took a taxi out to the rue Victorie? Would he be there? Perhaps he wouldn't like to feel pursued. I would like to send him a little present. But what? He needs so much . . . Perhaps he is as anxious to be in touch with me as I am to be in touch with him, and he is afraid to make a move because of Helmut. After all, I am a married woman. And Otto wouldn't like it either. I wonder: does Jean-Claude really like me? Am I really special for him?

I find it intolerable to have something on my mind incessantly, something that will not give way to anything else. It has never happened to me before to be obsessed by anyone or anything. I wonder if such a condition is normal, or if it is a function of what Dr Friedman diagnosed as my melancholia? And I am worried by my feeling that Jean-Claude felt sorry for me. Did he 'entertain' me out of a feeling of pity? Sometimes I feel that Helmut married me only out of pity: if he hadn't, who would have done? It's all something to do with the way I look. I am not womanly, I am told.

I fall asleep weeping. In the morning my cheeks are tight with dried tears.

Helmut takes me for a walk in the Bois de Boulogne before luncheon at La Cascade. I am grateful for the silence in the woods, and to breathe fresh air. And here there is no need for any guidebook, no need to take in dates and comment on the disposition of the trees. Over luncheon Helmut tells me that Jean-Claude is having an overture performed at the Club d'Essai the following week.

'Such a pity we shan't be here for it. I've no doubt you would have enjoyed the occasion. On the other hand, it may be for the best. Otto will want to feel he is Jean-Claude's most important guest.'

'Is he famous? Jean-Claude, I mean?'

'Hardly, dearest. The famous are usually rather better off.'

Nothing changes on the surface of Helmut's and my life. I continue to play my part at dinner, at the theatre and the opera. My part, directed by Helmut, is that of a decorative *ingénue*. I am to make his business associates feel welcome and interesting. I am to avoid talking about myself and to listen keenly to others discussing themselves. 'That is what gives people the greatest pleasure.' Above all, I am not to express a political view – I had none – or mention the price of anything.

I need such instruction. Although I played hostess in my father's house after my mother died, Father never brought his business life home. He stuck to lunching his customers, when the occasion so demanded, at the local hotel. Only at Christmas did he hold a cocktail party, organized by outside caterers, at home. He sent invitations to his most important customers and their wives, and took the opportunity to introduce them to some of the dignitaries of our small town – the bank manager, the vicar, my old headmistress and others. For this party Father liked to see me in a new dress. He never told me how to behave, what to say and what not to say. He said it was a pleasure to watch me step so easily into Mother's manner. I suppose I had watched her when I was little, and because she was so loving and so encouraging I had wanted to be just like her.

I quite enjoy perfecting the role in which Helmut casts me. It is a foolproof disguise. In it I am both pitied and envied, and neither response is appropriate and neither touches me. My real self is the lover of Jean-Claude. And so it is that I find myself perfecting one role while starting to learn the part for another. As Helmut's wife I am aware I am little more than a construction of his imagination. As Jean-Claude's lover I stop to wonder whether he is a construction of my own.

Park Terrace has become a hostile place, cold

and impersonal. It holds no charm for me at all. I seem to be wandering through its rooms like a wind-up toy lurching through a pre-ordained, limited routine.

A month or so after our return from Paris, Helmut leaves for New York. I am fearful he will insist that I accompany him. I am frantic to be alone with no obligations to fulfil and no role to play.

Something in me stirs. Something new. I have only myself to consider. With the whole day to myself and the nights, too, I enrol for French lessons. I had refused to learn French at school. It seemed so pointless then. Now it seems not only relevant but essential, for I want to write to Jean-Claude. In the meantime, before I feel competent to compose a letter in French, I receive one from him. It is a long letter, but couched simply enough for me to decipher. He writes that he thinks of me continually. He has tried for four months to get me out of his thoughts, but the intimacy of our meeting was so compelling he could not but believe that we are destined to be together. Disturbingly, he tells me that my life in London is meaningless, that I have been cast in the role of a rich roué's toy. I merit a better part. I am surprised by this part of his letter and wonder whether I have mistranslated it. All I read seems to add up to Jean-Claude's feeling that he has a mission to save me from a worthless life sentence.

I carry the letter with me for days, thinking over every word. I need to be sure of what I am replying to. I do so want to express my feelings. But they are confused – the more so since hearing from him. I must write in good, clear, unambiguous French. I don't want to run the risk of adding to my apparent childishness, to the appearance I give of being a victim . . .

In my reply I admit that I too wish to be with him. However, I do not feel I have that right. I am married to a decent man and cannot bring myself to cause chaos in his life, and hurt him. I go on to explain that I am physically rather fragile, and barren, and that Helmut provides me with a life that is suitably unstrenuous. I acknowledge that 'we all want many things to which we are not entitled'. I put down as sincerely as I can that I regret nothing, and that my night with him was the most beautiful of my life. At the end of my letter I add what, unbeknown to me, was to prove the decisive line. I say that when next I visit Paris I shall return to the rue Victorie and clean out the attic for him. According to Jean-Claude it was this thoughtful intention that decided my future. In the past, concern for his domestic comfort was something shown by his sister. My affectionate suggestion moved him to slot me into the chasm left by her untimely death.

Nevertheless, he does not reply very promptly to my letter. I am left wondering whether I have said the right things and used the right words. When eventually he does write back he says he was touched by my letter. He comments that my style is somewhat *cérémonieux* but that he was able to read between the lines. He is delighted I am learning French.

I have regained my strength. I am feeling rather well. I walk daily in Hyde Park and swim at my club in Berkeley Square. I lunch with the new friends I have made at my French class, and in the afternoons I seek out French films. London has become a quite congenial place for me, and a distraction from the long sob of loss which always accompanies me. I think a great deal about loss. I think mine is for something I have never quite had.

I am sure that had Mother not died when I was twelve I should never have entered into marriage with Helmut. Mother would have understood that I needed a marriage and not an alliance. I do not blame Father for pushing me into marriage. I can see that he would have wanted to avoid the unfair accusation that he was keeping me at home, by his side, for his own comfort and convenience. He was not a selfish man but he needed to feel that I was going to be as secure elsewhere as I was with him, under his roof. Had Mother lived, she would not only have wanted more for me but been able to bear less for herself.

I loved her so much that ever since she died I have not been able to think about her without searing pain, such pain as to make me decide to avoid consciously thinking about her at all. She was a quiet, pretty woman who liked nothing better than to sit and sew at the window, to raise her eyes to watch the passers-by, and drop them to continue her fine smocking on my next dress. She was simple in her demands. Quiet order was what she most cherished. She was impervious to the lure of money and position. Outward appearances meant nothing to her. She could easily have persuaded Father into buying a grander house, but she loved the house to which Father had brought her as a young bride and wanted nothing better. She and Father were devoted. Throughout my childhood I never heard a raised voice or saw a tear.

All this harmony and warmth was shattered when Mother died. The foundations of my life crumbled. Father was kind but had no idea of how to mother a girl of twelve, and I had no idea of what it was I needed. All the while I was growing up it was as if my amputated feelings had the power to cause me pain.

Had Mother lived, she would certainly have concerned herself with my physical condition, seen to it that I got to the right doctors. Taken me up to London to a teaching hospital. It is more likely than not that, had my condition been diagnosed early enough, it could have been put right. With Mother alive, I should perhaps have made a love-match and had children, and she would have joyously played a part in such a happy circumstance. All that was ordinary, unexciting but filled with meaning dissolved with Mother's death.

All streams of loss combine at a single confluence. Mother's death and Jean-Claude's absence connected. On the other hand, whereas Father had engineered my marriage to Helmut, I was in control of my French lessons and making new friends. Helmut is delighted with the new me, delighted with the progress I seem to be making on all fronts. He says I am 'coming out of myself', and I heard him boasting to a friend that my French is already more colloquial than his. 'And clever little Opal has managed to make it sound more Belgian or Swiss than English. In the normal way, sounding like either is not something I recommend, but in her case it works rather well.'

I know that the very fact of a French lover – whether past, present or beckoning – is adding to my sense of myself. If I never see Jean-Claude again (Heaven forfend!), our brief encounter will always make my circumstances more poignant.

It is November. The weather is frightful. We have been condemned to weeks of freezing fog. Throughout the country there have been rail and road accidents of unusual proportions, and an appalling wreck off the south coast in which many men's lives were lost. One evening when Helmut and I are uncharacteristically at home – we have turned down an invitation, not wanting to have to brave the cold and fog – the telephone rings and Helmut asks me to answer it. It is immediately clear to me that the call is long distance. For a split second I both hope and dread it may be Jean-Claude. An icy chill rises in me and my mouth dries. It is not Jean-Claude. It is the police at Dover. Do I know a French national by the name of Jean-Claude Guérigny? He has landed without money. He has given Mr and Mrs Helmut Gressinger as his hosts . . . Would I and my husband be willing to take responsibility for him? Unless one of us collects Mr Guérigny forthwith, he will be kept in the cells overnight and sent back to France on the first ferry tomorrow morning. Yes, conditions at sea are treacherous and Mr Guérigny is not feeling well after his crossing.

I assure the police that Mr Guérigny will be collected just as soon as we can arrange for a car. Will the police please bear in mind that the roads are particularly dangerous this evening and the journey to Dover may take longer than usual?

Helmut rings through to the chauffeur's cottage and asks Page to collect Jean-Claude. But before he leaves for Dover he is to call in for a letter. Helmut writes to the police in reassuring tones: Mr Guérigny will not be a burden on the public purse but on his own.

Suddenly the last person in the world I wish

to see, let alone entertain as a house guest, is Jean-Claude.

'Go and get some rest, my dear. Page won't be back for at least five hours.'

I don't know what to say. Should I apologize to Helmut? Does he imagine this is my idea? What on earth are we going to do with Jean-Claude?

'I think I'll ring Otto.' Helmut sounds calm, even cheerful. Unfortunately, Otto is not at home. Helmut tries his number every half-hour until 3 a.m., when he realizes that Otto is probably away on official business in Africa.

I lie on my bed fully clothed and fall asleep. When things are intractable I sleep soundly. Helmut rouses me rather brusquely when his final attempt to get hold of Otto fails. 'I'm going to bed now. You wait up for Jean-Claude.'

I had asked Mrs Page to make up the bed in the spare room on the upper floor – the quietest room, overlooking the gardens at the rear of the house. I sit in the study with the door ajar so that I shall hear the approaching car. My feelings of joyous expectation, of desire, of mystery, desert me. Suddenly all matters are practical ones and I feel anxious, irritable and apprehensive. It seems as if the course of my life is being diverted without my being consulted. This is the last circumstance in the world for which I have laid plans. This is not a scenario I want. And there is no one with whom to discuss it all. No one to give me any advice. It does show up how useless my relationship with Helmut is. Jean-Claude's action is making my marriage seem as farcical as he dubbed it.

Jean-Claude embraces me. I surrender. Utterly. The scent of his hair, his mellifluous French, his close embrace so that I can feel his body from his shoulders to his thighs, it all throws me back to the rue Victorie. I am hypnotized.

'I had to see you. Both for my sake and your own.'

I draw him along the corridor into the kitchen. All he wants is tea and toast. He is ashen. Then he asks for brandy. He is dishevelled and tired. His clothes – the same ones he was wearing when I met him – look cheap and worn in Park Terrace. He is outraged and barely coherent, at having been arrested and confined for eight hours in a filthy police cell. On and on he rages about the British, who imagine themselves so superior . . . the disgusting food he was offered, which he did not touch, the ugliness of Dover. As for the law! So, he had no money! Was that a crime? While he rants I think of other things. What am I going to do with him? On the one hand he has taken the liberty of invading my privacy. On the other, is this not what I want? I look closely at Jean-Claude. I see he does not belong here in Park Terrace. I have never really felt I belonged here, either.

The police have given him permission to stay for five days. He must stay in London. He shows me the form specifying the dates and stating the penalty for outstaying his welcome: Helmut Gressinger will be liable for a fine of £2,000 and Jean-Claude will be put in prison.

I take him up to his room and run a bath for him. He hardly speaks now. He keeps trying to catch hold of my arm, my hand, to kiss me. I can see that he does understand something of the quandary in which he has placed me, but clearly he is too tired to talk about it now. I switch off the taps and say good-night. 'I look forward to seeing you in the morning,' I lie.

Helmut is on the telephone when I come downstairs in the morning. It is Saturday. We usually go to a gallery or do some shopping in Bond Street on Saturday mornings, and lunch at the Caprice. I can see, however, that Helmut is making other plans for this Saturday. He is booking a seat on a plane to Zurich. It takes off at midday. 'I've some business to attend to in Switzerland. I think this situation is one you'd better deal with yourself,' he tells me, adding that he will be away for a week. I realize he has seen the form from the police that I left on his desk last night and he has calculated that I shall have got rid of Jean-Claude by then.

I find myself fussing with his packing over-attentively. By the time Page has the car at the front door there has been no sound from Jean-Claude's room. Helmut kisses me goodbye in his normal manner and says he hopes things will go smoothly and work out to everyone's satisfaction. There is not the slightest hint in his voice that he is put out or fears for the future. Jean-Claude is visiting; Jean-Claude will leave. Everything will revert to normal.

PARIS

He who loves and he whose desires are satisfied are not the same man.

Marcel Proust

I was never to know how Helmut reacted to finding the house empty on his return from Zurich. He did not reply to the letter I left on his desk until months later, by which time he must have overcome the initial shock my flight must surely have caused him. But I say 'must have' without real evidence: he never reproached me for my action. When in May, six months later, he came to Paris and took me to the Tour d'Argent for lunch, he passed me an envelope. 'Don't open it here. Wait till you're alone.' And when I was alone, in the Metro, I found a contract to sign. Helmut was going to transfer so much a month into a bank account for me and I could draw it out at an office in the Champs-Elysées. It was a very modest sum for Helmut. I had not asked him for anything, nor had I expected anything. This contract was, perhaps, the only evidence from which I could deduce Helmut's hurt. By giving me a little he was showing both concern for me and his determination that I should pay materially for what I had done to him. Perhaps, too, he may have believed that once the gloss on my love affair dimmed, his money would

43

act as a reminder of the comforts to which I could return.

I did not know it at the time, but Helmut knew that Jean-Claude was still seeing Otto. Of course I knew he saw Otto, but not what those visits implied, and Helmut – whether from loyalty to his friend or on account of some sort of inhibition in relation to me – never hinted at anything improper. My naïveté, my lack of experience, may have protected me from what would have been obvious to anyone else. But even had I been told something of the nature of their relationship, I am not sure that I would have understood or believed, or felt betrayed.

The hardships in the attic were ones with which I coped easily. The lack of space, the cold, the absence of hot water – all these contingencies I negotiated with the skills I had acquired in domestic science (my best subject) and as a Girl Guide. I was twenty-three. I had been accustomed to comfort all my life. No doubt Helmut assumed I should be incapable of adjusting to discomfort. According to conventional wisdom, it is more of a strain to give up something than it is to endure, never having known it. But living with Jean-Claude convinced me that this is flawed thinking. Because my experience was not of being poor, the discomforts of the poverty that I had to put up with in the rue Victorie did not suggest themselves as unending.

For Jean-Claude, who had always been abjectly poor, there seemed no way of escaping a hand-to-mouth existence by his own efforts: only a miracle could effect it. (Maybe I appeared as that miracle?) He was thirty-three. He suffered from chronic bronchitis and arthritis, conditions that sprang from the way he had had to live in war-torn France. Whereas for me the rigours of the Second World War meant two ounces of butter a week and five inches of bathwater, for Jean-Claude they had involved near-starvation on a diet of turnips – and the dangers of being on the run. Since the end of hostilities he had had a permanent roof over his head, but no other aspect of his life had improved radically, whereas I had been passed from a doting father to a doting husband.

When Jean-Claude and I quit Park Terrace we did so with tea-chests packed with valuables of mine, largely selected by him from many more than we could manage to take. Among the items Jean-Claude chose were antiquarian books given to me by Helmut in the expectation that my reading horizons, which stretched no further than the English classics, might be enlarged by beautiful print and binding and lavish illustrations, and a collection of now rare pre-war recordings of the Beethoven quartets and the song-cycles of Schumann and Schubert recorded in private performances. I was surprised by the selection of items Jean-Claude made from my wardrobe. (And rather shocked that he helped himself to two of Helmut's silk scarves. I said nothing. Helmut had eighteen others.) I could not imagine when I should have occasion to wear some of my more exotic outfits. They would have no practical use in the rue Victorie. However, I trusted Jean-Claude when he said it would be lovely to have the Epstein bust of a child and the little Vuillard etching, two of Mother's most precious belongings. I trusted him to see that I was equipped for the new life I had chosen.

And I believe I did choose this new life, that I was not coerced. I made a decision for myself, possibly the first big one I ever made. Of course, had Helmut not left for Zurich but stayed at Park Terrace, and had the situation between the three of us then become something of a tussle, I might have lacked the courage finally to pack up and return to Paris with Jean-Claude. As it was, with Helmut gone, Jean-Claude had the time to convince me that my life in London not only lacked quality but was something of a farce.

'Your husband may well be decent, kind and generous to you, but all you are to him is a decorative object. You're not a partner. I wouldn't be at all surprised if he insured you on his household policy along with his antiquities, paintings and Persian rugs.'

I had felt useless in Park Terrace. The domestic skills I had acquired at school and perfected looking after Father when Mother died, were not skills valued by Helmut. They were for servants. But I had not been raised to be merely decorative. Indeed, I have every reason to believe that Father did not regard me as decorative at all. He was old-fashioned, and had been lucky to find a woman as old-fashioned as himself. I was brought up to be useful to a man. For this purpose it was not necessary for me to stay on at school after I was sixteen and attend university. And as soon as I settled in the rue Victorie, I discovered I was very useful indeed.

We slipped quickly into a routine. When I look back, it seems remarkable how quickly. It was as if a couple of animals hounded from one burrow, nest or lair had immediately taken possession of another and started up just where they had left off.

I was no longer to be an article of decoration, however. My appearance, which Helmut had embellished with jewellery, expensive clothes and regular visits to beauty salons, Jean-Claude liked unadorned and without make-up. My presence, which Helmut claimed only when business lent him time, Jean-Claude demanded constantly. Indeed, he was nervous when I was out of the attic. Every morning I went to buy a *baguette* at Bluot's *boulangerie* at the corner of the road. It took me no more than five minutes there and back. But when I pushed open the gate into the yard on my return, I always saw Jean-Claude at the window.

I was not bored, not in the least. Having to prepare our food on a couple of electric rings was a challenge I enjoyed. I kept a notebook of what

I made each day. I did not want to repeat myself too often. I invented a means of preparing four dishes at once. I had two saucepans, one containing a stew of some sort, the other pasta or potatoes. Above each, in a colander or sieve, I would steam a vegetable and a pudding. Jean-Claude had never tasted steamed puddings before and he liked them. I tried never to throw any food away. I made toast from left-over bits of *baguette* and always kept a kettle on the hob. When I looked after Father I had all the modern equipment I needed. In the rue Victorie, lacking a refrigerator, I had to make do with the window-sill and milk- and butter-coolers. Lacking an oven, I discovered that a joint of beef could be deep-fried with excellent results. I found that in France it was the practice to buy meat, fruit, vegetables and bread daily (in the case of bread, at least twice daily) oneself, rather than rely on deliveries once or twice a week. This worked well for me. It forced me out of the attic three times a day to discover my new surroundings and meet the local people.

I had never been happier. For the first time in my life I had a lover who was a companion. Throughout the day he would stop work, make us coffee and talk to me about what he was working on, what he was reading and what I was doing. When I had been in the attic long enough to have tidied and cleaned the cupboards, and put a shine on the ancient chest of drawers and wardrobe, I settled to knit Jean-Claude sweaters and socks.

When I took my knitting to the window and sat working there, I thought of Mother. I was glad to be a little like her.

Reine les Falaises is neither town nor country. But it is nothing like English suburbia. More like a village within a town. I loved it. I came to know it with my eyes shut, by its noises and its smells. I felt safe there. Jean-Claude would never accompany me on my explorations. For him, Reine was the burnt, dry and tasteless edge of a tasty pie. He preferred, he said, to submerge himself in the urban swill, or be in deep country. And the streets of Reine held memories for him he preferred not to recall. People who knew the whole Guérigny family would be bound to stop him and ask him questions he did not want to face. For him, Reine was numbing. For me it was exhilarating.

Our house stood at the east end of the rue Victorie, where the shops give way to workshops. Five identical houses, four storeys of sad, grey stone, stood behind ten-foot iron grilles. Beyond, towards open country, the pavements widened for a mile and blackthorn hedges, brambles, old man's beard and nettles concealed little strips of garden, ribbons of green, bordered by hydrangeas, leading to fanciful *pavillons*. From the front attic window we could see down the rue de Fleuve to the river. The rue de Fleuve is a steep, narrow lane with the church on one side behind iron palings and on the other the graveyard behind chalky walls held together with ivy. An ever-present but barely detectable white dust hung in the air of Reine les Falaises – a reminder of how this *quartier* had acquired its name. A few yards before the rue de Fleuve joined the tow-path along the Seine, it was traversed by the Cours Mirabeau, a wide boulevard lined with pollarded lime trees where the daily market was held.

I loved the market. I loved its moods. Lying low beside the river, it could be misty, it could be translucent. No chalky dust hung about the stalls. I was introduced to an art form that did not exist in England. I had gone, as the doctor had ordered, where I could feast my senses. Polished pyramids of apples and pears, still-life arrangements of humble carrots and potatoes, hillocks of pale butter topped with parsley trees, cut flowers in superannuated tins green-painted – and a cast of salesmen who in England would have found employment only once a year, in pantomime. I watched the butcher with particular fascination. Holding a joint of beef before him on an outstretched arm, he would wave his free hand over its surface in a gesture approaching a mystical rite, conferring upon the excellence of his merchandise a value far in excess of what the none-too-prosperous housewives of Reine hoped to pay.

'*Mesdames! Regardez-vous bien!* What quality! And where on the face of this earth would you find such an exceptional price? Such value . . .'

'It's a disgrace . . . What does he take us for, how am I to feed a family of six?' They consulted one another, hardly hoping for advice but grateful to vent their anger, grateful that all were of one mind. Then came the consultation proper, and the bargaining began.

In winter the chestnut-seller installed himself at the edge of the market. While he fanned his charcoal-burner with bellows he gossiped to a gaggle of old women who gathered to warm themselves around his patch. He knew everyone, and their business, and he made it his. He was eighty; he had occupied this patch since he was a boy and he had seen it all: drunks, thieves, prostitutes. Good times and bad times. He had heard the complaints of women in labour, and the groans of pleasure that were a prelude to their misery. 'They don't know what they want, not the young ones,' he observed to his audience. And the old women cackled agreement.

In the early 1950s it was illegal for a foreigner to work in France without a permit. Indeed, mere permission to reside in that country for more than three weeks was strictly limited and one had to satisfy the authorities that one would not become a burden on the state. When I went to the office of the Prefect of Police to apply for a *permis de séjour*, the police were not impressed by my verbal assurances. They insisted upon coming out to Reine to inspect my living accommodation, and the person with whom I shared it. That done, they were less impressed than ever. They pronounced

51

the attic unfit for human habitation and Jean-Claude inadequate to support me. One officer suggested behind his hand that I visit him at his home after work, and in exchange for this little attention he would write me a six-month *permis de séjour*. When I refused him, he reluctantly – on the evidence of my bank account – wrote me out permission for four weeks, with the proviso that I return to his office every four weeks . . . He knew well the anxiety this would create as I wondered whether one day he would turn me away. Fortunately, after a few months, this officer was replaced by a more avuncular figure and the threat receded.

During this period of uncertainty, Jean-Claude was as anxious as I. He never missed the opportunity to tell me how different his life had become since I moved in with him: he was happy now, he could work.

I revelled in the routine of this life. Our day started with my brewing coffee with the beans Jean-Claude ground, and buttering lengths of *baguette* to drunk. When Jean-Claude had finished his breakfast, he walked down the lane by the side of the house in his old dressing-gown and felt slippers. In the rain, he walked under an umbrella with broken spokes; in the snow, in haste. He washed and shaved at his parents' *pavillon*. Once a week he bathed there. I was not given the run of the *pavillon* and I took it that, since I had not been extended this facility, I was not welcome to it. I was surprised at first that

Jean-Claude bathed so infrequently. I learnt that a weekly bath was the norm in France among the poor. Indeed, when I happened to mention to Mme Guérigny that in England I bathed daily, she sniffed, making me feel there was something profligate and indecent in such luxury. 'Total immersion is debilitating,' she told me, adding: 'It destroys the muscles of the breast.' When I recounted this to Jean-Claude, he said that innocent peasants regarded frequent bathing as some sort of health precaution, associated with the depravity of the city.

Jean-Claude made his telephone calls from his parents' *pavillon*. The little house was empty in the mornings, of course. M. and Mme Guérigny did not return from market until just before one o'clock. I never knew to whom Jean-Claude spoke or with whom he made rendezvous. From the beginning, I never asked and he never said. This secrecy made me feel cold and lonely. There was nothing in my own life that I could not confide to him, and I could not imagine what there might be in his that he needed to keep from me. I knew he loved and needed me, but the fact that while I washed up, scrubbed, cleaned and tidied for us both he was making contact with people I had never met, would never meet, and whose names I did not know, formed a cloud over my days. Of course, there were times when it lifted altogether, and many times when I was not aware of it. But there were also times when it descended low.

It was a help when I received letters. Jean-Claude

would return with the mail after he had shaved. Letters could take my mind off most things. Jean, the housemaid, wrote regularly. Helmut irregularly. Olga, and one or two old friends still living in my home town, kept in touch. But Father had been so upset by my bolting that he never wrote. I wrote to him, though. I tried my hardest to explain how it had come about. But I never really expected him to understand and sympathize. Perhaps, had he not been so ill, he would have come round. I did not learn how ill he had become until too late. Helmut went to see him in hospital. He wrote saying there was no point in my coming over: Father was in a coma. He had tried to explain things to him from my point of view . . . There's no getting away from it, Helmut was an unusual man.

However, I was in no doubt that I had done the right thing by leaving him. I was deeply in love with Jean-Claude, and the difference between how I felt towards him and how I felt towards Helmut convinced me that it would have been dishonest, even distasteful, to go on living my married life. Jean-Claude was my ruling passion. My whole existence was devoted to pleasing him. I felt an affinity with him. There was nothing he said that I did not recognize as being the expression of my own heart. I mean, nothing he said about us. And all the time, when my eyes were on him, I desired him. And when we were apart and my thoughts were about him, my body absorbed my mind's obsession and throbbed for him.

I was taken by surprise by my feelings. I had never experienced anything remotely like this before. At first it had been his physical beauty, then the cast of his mind. Finally, it was because he wanted me to be part of his world of music. There was an erotic madness between us, a raging appetite for one another assuaged only by its being renewed. But because I was young and inexperienced I mistook the nature of our relationship, and came to understand it only after it was well behind me.

At the time I believed that I surrendered completely to him but that he did not surrender completely to me. I sensed, without understanding the implications, that he had areas of being upon which I was forbidden to encroach. I interpreted his secrecy as emotional avarice. Indeed, had he told me where he went and with whom on the evenings he spent away from the attic, I should have felt less vulnerable: it was secrecy itself I found hostile. It never occurred to me that he was protecting me. I simply regarded these absences as a lesson, a foretaste of what it would be like when they became a permanence. I was ruled in those days by insecurity. Mother had disappeared without warning. Father had rejected me and died. Helmut had made no effort to restrain me from leaving him. It seemed that the thread linking me to those with whom I was familiar was inherently insubstantial. And death stalked that attic.

★   ★   ★

Every Sunday, having visited her daughter's grave, Mme Guérigny served lunch for her family: her two much older brothers and their wives, her husband, Jean-Claude and me. Whatever her feelings towards her family, she was my reluctant hostess and I was her reluctant guest. My inclusion was a concession wrung from Mme G by Jean-Claude. We were, after all, living in sin, and she was a devoted Catholic.

We forgathered at one o'clock for a glass of Suze, a bitter aperitif which was probably made from artichokes because the label on the bottle carried a picture of one. We sat down to lunch at one-fifteen and rose sometime after three-thirty. To my mind, the meal was astonishingly plenteous. So much was still on ration or impossible to obtain in Britain. Had it not been for Helmut's wealth and his travels, we should not have had anything like the variety of food Mme Guérigny put on her table. Added to which, these were simple people who worked hard for modest sums of money. When there was a roast, invariably it would be preceded by a delicious soup. If, however, there was a slow-cooked casserole, there would first be an *hors-d'oeuvre*. In either case, there was always a cheese (just one, and that *à point*) and, to finish, a *tarte* and cream.

The room in which we lunched was referred to as the 'salon'. In England, it would have been the parlour, and like the parlour, the salon was used only for entertaining visitors. M. and Mme Guérigny

56

lived the week long exclusively in the bedroom and kitchen, and only those two rooms were kept heated. The salon was never quite warm enough when we forgathered, not even in summer. A cold damp hung about the beechwood furniture and clung to the velour drapes. By the time we had finished the meal, this cool was somewhat camouflaged beneath the odour of food and the body heat of eight diners. Within an hour or so of our departure, I felt sure the proper chill had returned and would reign until the eight of us next dispelled it.

It would have been a consolation if I had found a mother in Mme Guérigny. I did not. My relationship with her was difficult. We did not take to one another; whatever the circumstances had been, I do not imagine we would have made friends. But in her tragic situation she clearly resented my being young and alive while her daughter was young and dead. She found it obnoxious that her son permitted himself a living relationship when, like her, he should be occupying himself exclusively with a dead one. From the start, she made it clear that as long as I could be of use to Jean-Claude she would tolerate me, but that my relationship with her son was in her gift and subject to her approval, and this might not always be forthcoming. Mme Guérigny, whilst relying on her son, still found it distasteful that he was managing to survive in the face of the family tragedy.

There was no way I could know just what passed between Mme G and her son when they were together and alone. I believe they entered into a sort of conspiracy to keep alive Montaine's existence when no one else was around to dissipate her spectral control. In company, with another or others, they would bank down the embers of the past. One might embark upon a conversation and find it quite suddenly rounded off before it got under way. One might mention an object or a locality, and sepulchral silence would descend. Montaine's entire existence belonged to Mme Guérigny and Jean-Claude, and every detail of it, everything that was even remotely reminiscent of it, was in their custody.

This exclusivity did not include M. Guérigny. I never heard his wife or son exchange more than a few words with him. He was obviously a sad man, but in his soundlessness I detected a stillness that neither his wife nor his son achieved. I used to watch him out of the back attic window in the late afternoon, when he had risen from his rest. The garden was his domain; he had his rabbits to feed and the birds to admonish for ravaging his cherry trees. He smiled in the garden. He was not estranged from animals and birds. Once, I saw him out in his nightshirt. He looked pathetic, but I was unmoved. Indeed, I was disgusted by the sight of his blanched legs, skinny, with blue knots of varicose veins. He was standing looking up as usual into his trees, but he was scratching his backside. And he spat. I never saw Mme Guérigny in the garden. I never saw the two of them in conversation. I heard him ask her to pass the salt and I heard her tell him to fill the van with petrol and unpack the crates – nothing more than that. I asked Jean-Claude whether things had been different, once, between them.

'Well, perhaps, before the war . . . before . . . you understand.'

I could not ask further questions. I had learnt the rules. But it seemed to me that, had they loved one another well, they would have been able to support one another in their tragedy. I wondered what it was that could come between a husband and wife when their child killed herself away from home and in circumstances for which they could not hold themselves in any way responsible. I do not believe that M. Guérigny did feel responsible. I believe his lasting sadness was to observe the devastation of his wife. It seemed that she, on the other hand, had felt implicated. I wondered whether she felt she had encouraged the too-close relationship between Jean-Claude and Montaine, in an effort to keep her children children?

Certainly, Montaine's death had affected her in a dramatic and all-embracing way. Earlier in life she had loved music passionately, but after Montaine's suicide she had never listened to another note. Not even the notes composed by her son. When performances of Jean-Claude's work were due to be broadcast, he would leave her a message with details of the time and date. Next day he would find the little piece of paper screwed up in the waste-paper basket and the matter ignored. Nor did Mme Guérigny visit the cinema or theatre, or drop in on a neighbour. She had loved to go to the music-hall when first she moved to Paris and she had made friends in the *quartier*. Nor would she go away on holiday – and heaven knows, she needed a rest. It was as if, by staying at home continuously, without distraction, she would not risk missing the return of Montaine. The only people in whose company she would sit were those who came to Sunday lunch and were also waiting for Montaine's return.

Conversation over Sunday lunch was dominated by the uncles, Gaston and Marius. Gaston was a fishmonger who left evidence of his occupation on every hand he shook. Marius was a horse butcher. I never saw him in his bloodstained overalls, but I always imagined him thus in my mind. Both men had shops in a village ten miles to the east of Reine, on the Seine. Both were heavy red-wine drinkers, always bloated, and each jealously guarded his own *inferior* status. Whereas Gaston had managed to buy a small boat to go fishing, Marius had not so much as managed the purchase of two matching garden chairs. Whereas the wife of one had afforded a new hat, the wife of the other was short of sous for knitting-wool. Their sparring for position of least-favoured son gave me pause for thought. However, they combined in boundless enthusiasm for their local soccer *équipe*, and for their local newspaper. Every Sunday they rehearsed the contents of the previous week's editions. On one occasion, when unexpectedly Mme Guérigny was giving her views an airing, I was asked for mine, and handed the page under discussion. I cannot remember the subject involved. What I do remember, however, is my unease when I noticed an advertisement at the foot of the page: *Anti-semitic pamphlets sent post-free to interested readers*. I had a nasty feeling that Mme Guérigny's sisters-in-law, Agnes and Agathe, might well be 'interested'. It had been from their lips that I first heard ushered the expression *avare comme un juif*, followed by a vicious attack on the only Jewish family in their village to have survived the war and returned to claim their old house. The general feeling at table was that they were luckier than they deserved.

I knew quite a bit about the war and the suffering of the peoples of Europe. Father had met Helmut when I was small. It was in connection with getting refugee children out of Germany. Mother and Father, through their church, were arranging for Jewish children to be taken in by local families. They themselves invited a little girl to share my bedroom for a while. (She did not stay long; an uncle of hers turned up and took her to live with him in Manchester.) Although Father and Helmut did business with one another, it was their work for refugees that brought them close and endeared Helmut to Mother and Father. They talked all the time about danger and oppression. I may not have understood everything I heard at the time, but later it all slotted into place. After the war, when Helmut had something to do with a factory in Brazil, where he and Father had managed to set up a colony of displaced persons, Father supplied all the machine tools and worked closely with Helmut on the project. I received a strong impression that it was not enough to know about injustice and suffering; practical solutions had to be found.

I was shocked by what I heard. I wanted to object but I did not know how to do so. I worked that out only much later, when it was too late. I looked over at Jean-Claude, hoping he might say something. He did not.

These lunches, a dutiful ritual, were overseen by an outsize photograph of Montaine, whose name was assiduously avoided. I used to wonder how these people could resist talking about her. She had been precious to each of them. She had been beautiful, gifted and, from all reports, charming. I would watch the brothers sparring and the women, heads down, picking into their food with a concentration more usually associated with ruminants, and wonder how this family had cohered in the past. Who had been its head? Today I could not decide whether it was the absent Montaine or the *pot au feu*.

It was in the summer, some six months after I had arrived in Paris, that I determined to earn a little money. We needed more than I had. Jean-Claude kept mentioning things he wanted. And a job would get me out of the attic. However, it seemed to me that an insurmountable problem presented itself: I had no qualifications. As it transpired, this was no problem at all; rather, it was a benefit. If I had had qualifications I should not have been able to use them legally, and I should have been too hoity-toity to take on the sort of menial, unregulated work available.

Within weeks of my arrival, Mme Bluot at the bakery had asked me whether I would consider giving her son Didier English conversation lessons. Didier had not taken to a foreign language and was having trouble keeping up in class. I said I would think about it, never for a minute believing that I was qualified to take a pupil. And then there was the problem of Jean-Claude. I had noticed something puzzling. From time to time, Jean-Claude would take his motor cycle and ride into the city to pass the evening with Otto or some nameless, unspecified friend. On these occasions he was perfectly happy to leave me alone in the attic. But when I needed a breath of air, or wished to explore Reine, and was out of the attic for an hour or so, leaving him alone there, he became depressed and even a little disagreeable.

I waited, hoping for an opportune moment to discuss the possibility of my earning a little money. None arose. And then, one day, out of the blue, Jean-Claude mentioned that if he had a piano he might take pupils. 'Shall we buy one?' I suggested, and then went on to say that I might find a job.

Didier was eleven, a quiet child with the natural distrust of foreigners peculiar to the French of his class, and times. I put forward the idea to Mme Bluot that, rather than sit either side of a table, reminding Didier of school and his failure to keep up, he and I would do better to talk down by the river, in the park, even in the Café du Coin. Twice a week I collected my pupil from the bakery after school. Mme Bluot would put a couple of *petits pains au chocolat* in a greaseproof bag, and Didier and I would set out to explore Reine. We would go down to the Seine and speak of water, boats and fish; or we would go to the public park, where a few birds languished in an ancient aviary and the old mynah bird entertained us with a lavish range of endearments. Sometimes we went to the Cours Mirabeau and watched the debris from the daily market being picked over by the local dogs. Didier had class-mates who lived in the extensive nineteenth-century houses, set back in their own grounds, on the hill behind the rue Victorie. The cupolas and weather-vanes that garnished these imposing mansions pierced the pure blue skies on blameless days, and on others became shrouded in mist and cloud. It occurred to me, when I got to know some of these families, that they really might believe that their position on the hill placed them nearer to heaven than the less privileged folk below. It was mostly merchants who lived here, but notwithstanding their love of luxury, their houses were gloomy inside. I did not know what to make of these people until, years later, I read the novels of François Mauriac.

Didier hardly noticed how quickly he came to understand and speak English. I made it a rule – which, it is true, he broke from time to time when he had something particularly pressing or intimate to convey – that he should not drop into French while we were together. Mme Bluot was most impressed when she heard Didier enter the shop, prattling in a language she did not understand. And I was delighted to have the neighbourhood laid out for me in the way a child sees its domain, and to earn a little money and receive from Mme Bluot the excellent unsold cakes and breads she would otherwise have had Didier feed to the ducks.

At the end of the rue Victorie, past the Café du Coin, was a road I rarely took alone, and never with Didier. The stucco on the houses that rose like cliffs of grey stone in the rue de Sèvres was enough to depress me in itself, blotched as it was with building acne, let alone the drains blocked with refuse and the greasy pipes round which foaming suds slept fitfully. It seemed that danger lurked in the ever-present shadows. The stench of poverty and neglect was stitched to the wind in this narrow crevice. The blinds of the houses were always drawn to different levels, since each of the rooms was let to a different lodger, and their times of getting up and going to bed were different. Notices on the gates that swung loose on broken hinges read *Attention au Chien.* Yet it was hard to imagine a burglar visiting the rue de Sèvres: I rather imagined that this would be where he lived. The backyards of the houses in this road faced on to a canal. From the far bank, I saw little waste-lands chock-full of old tin baths, rungless ladders, wheel-less bicycles, pecking chickens and, in one, an old sow. Didier was forbidden by M. and Mme Bluot to visit the rue de Sèvres. He did not know that Mme Bluot had asked me not to walk in that direction ('It is a street so disreputable, madame, it could lead a child astray.'), and so he frequently tried conducting me that way. I asked him why he so dearly wished to walk in a street as dank as a sewer, and to play by the waters of an oily, rat-infested canal, when we had the exquisite reaches of the Seine at hand, and the gardens of his school friends.

'To see the trash!' he told me with childlike frank-ness. He said there were *putains* there, with their *maquereaux*. I did not see the value in teaching him the English equivalents of these words, and merely reminded him to talk in English. It surprised me, nevertheless, that in such a small place as Reine there existed a street so out of character with the rest. A blind alley, poor, stinking and threatening: a little corner of squalor.

'The deaf and dumb family lives there. They speak with their fingers and make disgusting noises. UGH! They are ridiculous!'

'Don't speak French, Didier!' I tried to impress upon the child that if he had landed in England before he met me, he would not have spoken English and people there might have regarded *him* as ridiculous. He fell silent for a while and then answered me apologetically – in English.

All proceeded uneventfully. Didier was happy to feed the ducks on the river and take me to visit his schoolteacher. He introduced me to the local shoemender, he showed me where the gypsies sometimes camped. We went together to the yard of an old man who bred worms for fishermen and bought a jarful for M. Bluot. Then, one afternoon, Didier led me down the rue de Fleuve to the cemetery.

It was pure chance that had brought Jean-Claude to the attic window that same afternoon. He caught sight of me descending the rue de Fleuve. Because he lost sight of me quickly, he knew that I could not be going down to the river or turning left into the church: he had an uninterrupted view of both. He guessed rightly that little Didier Bluot was leading me into the cemetery and would direct me to Montaine's grave.

'She killed herself,' Didier informed me casually. 'It was an affair of the heart,' he added cheerfully, no doubt quoting an adult. He spoke these words in French, and it was the French, somehow, that carried with it a particular poignancy for me. I am not sure that I listened to much more of what Didier had to recount on the subject of Montaine's death. I was hypnotized by the knowing way this eleven-year-old blurted out so unfeelingly a tragedy that had paralysed an entire family. Perhaps all the neighbours in Reine would respond similarly. Or was it the unvarnished cruelty of an eleven-year-old? Montaine's suicide had taken place two and a half years ago. I was beginning to understand from the people I had encountered in Reine that it was a drama still running, and likely to continue to run.

When I got back to the attic, Jean-Claude was waiting for me at the top of the stairs.

'Where the hell have you been?' he shouted. His face was bloodless and so too were his knuckles, clutching the banisters. 'Never! Never go there again!' He did not utter the word 'cemetery'. 'D'you hear me? Are you listening? Never! Never!' And then, beseechingly: 'Promise me you'll never go there again. I ask very little of you, Opal . . .'

I promised. I apologized. I told him that, of course, I would never knowingly do anything to hurt or upset him. I explained . . . I tried to explain. But he was not listening. 'Just don't go there again.'

I considered the 'very little' that Jean-Claude asked of me. I reflected upon it. It was a fact. I had so little to offer, nothing to turn to account.

I knew I was not clever. Proof positive: I had no qualifications. Nor was I well placed, not here in France. I had no contacts that might be of use to a composer. All I had were a few personal belongings and a little money, and these I gave to Jean-Claude with all my heart. Yes, I gave him my heart . . . and my body, put willingly and joyfully at his continual disposal, not only in a sexual way but as general factotum.

He left the attic, slamming the door behind him. I assumed he was off to his parents' *pavillon* to make a telephone call. I felt pierced to the heart, dejected and lonely. I went to the looking-glass and surveyed myself. I saw that my face, too, was whey-coloured, my hands rough and my hair dry. I looked like one of those peasant girls in the old folk-tales, the ones who never get to the ball. I was always sweeping, washing and cooking. What else could I do? Anyhow, I had no personal ambition. All I wanted was an exceptional career for Jean-Claude, for that was what he wanted for himself. I was glad that my presence, my little money, meant he did not have to carry messages across Paris on his motor cycle. It did not enter my head that I might have the seeds of a talent, that I too might have a career and that I should be preparing myself for it. Father had told me repeatedly that as a woman my role was to surrender to a man: that submission and compliance would be the meaning of my life. As a barren woman, boyish physically, and shy, I had not found meaning with Helmut. I had with Jean-Claude.

He had happened upon me at the crucial moment: I had little idea of who I was or what I was entitled to from life, let alone what it behoved me to contribute. I was naïve and I was bored. Jean-Claude saw in me an exotic combination of youth and money. I was in bud, not flower, clearly unfulfilled by my husband. It was a challenge. At the time, Jean-Claude was paralysed with grief, and much as he craved professional recognition, he had no idea how to pursue it. It was quite literally his vitality that had been sapped by Montaine's death, leaving his talent and his intelligence in irons without it. I believe he sensed he could unleash a drive in me that could propel him to recognition. As it transpired, he was right, but for the wrong reason. It was not my little money and the confidence he erroneously imagined it engendered that came briefly to his rescue, but my blind passion for him. He eased me into a role he had only half-consciously cast me for without my noticing it and, by emphasizing the physical attraction I had for him, he made me feel imperative. No other man had so eloquently and constantly spoken of the way I had haunted him from the first moment he cast eyes on me. And further, he said that it was his determination to see me again, to persuade me to live with him, that had strengthened in him the desire to go on living, a desire that had been weak since the death of Montaine.

'I cannot say why, precisely, but for hundreds, thousands – an infinite number of reasons – you fascinated me, and that fascination encouraged in me the desire to live, something that abandoned me on the death of my sister. The pointlessness of my existence – stealing money and food from my poor parents, wood from the railway cutting, begging my *coup de vin* from Suzanne at the Café du Coin – all that was clearly not worthy of me. You came, and provided out of love. I could work as I had before Montaine died. I said to myself: I shall write something monumental in memory of her. And you, Opal, you will exult in it because you made it possible.

'There was no reason for me to go on living. At first I did so to console Maman. I was sickened to see how Papa behaved. Montaine's death somehow served to glorify his conscience. In the event, Maman was inconsolable. She refused me the *pavillon* for a while because she discovered that in the evenings I met friends in town. She regarded this as an outrage, a desecration of Montaine's memory. It was disloyal that I was able to divert myself, but appalling that I did so with Otto. Now, *mon petit*, I can do everything. I can be myself again!'

So while his real need for me had something to do with practicalities, he reinforced in me the sense that his need had something to do with his sister's death. Had she lived, I felt sure he would not have had time for me. Montaine and I were not similar in any obvious way, but Jean-Claude may well have detected in me something of the quality he relied on in his sister. Something of that quality survived in me. No one else would have detected it. But no one else would have been looking for it.

Throughout her childhood, indeed until the day she died, Montaine had been the most important person in Jean-Claude's life. Her death opened a gap in his existence which threatened continually to devour him altogether. Since childhood in la Sologne – a part of France largely unknown to any but the French – where the two had roamed unfettered throughout years of sunlit days, their relationship never changed, never matured. Montaine was 'little mother' as well as *copain*. He was her responsibility as well as her playmate. These were the roles I was cast to take over.

I learnt – without making myself appear too inquisitive – that the Guérigny roots struck deep into la Sologne, a land whose finest hours had been in the twelfth and thirteenth centuries. It was only after the war that Jean-Claude's parents followed Mme Guérigny's brothers and their wives to Paris, the soil of la Sologne clinging to their boots. They were always to prefer that sandy, largely unregenerative soil to the cobbles and pavements they trod in the *banlieue* of Paris. They had made the move only for money. Because Jean-Claude hated to be questioned about anything relating to his family, I had to commit to memory every little detail he let slip. From these fragments I reconstructed the brooding melancholy of a land subject to disaster after disaster, a family forced out through poverty, and I wove from insubstantial vapour the misty quilt in which I sensed his childhood to have been enveloped.

To avoid his being rounded up by the Germans for STO *(Service du Travail Obligatoire)* and sent to the munitions factories in the east, Montaine and Mme Guérigny hid Jean-Claude in a sunken hollow in the grounds of a crumbling manor house at the edge of the village. (It was from the time of this incarceration that he developed his chest and joint complaints.) Montaine had helped Jean-Claude dig out the cave and make it impenetrable and impermeable. It had also fallen to Montaine to take her brother food when he was confined to the cave, warn him of danger when it was acute, and when the coast was clear to fetch him home. With the war over and M. Guérigny back from the front, the brother and sister became intoxicated with the experience of freedom. They passed four months just wandering about the countryside, pitching their tent, swimming in the numberless ponds that are a feature of the land, and living off game they shot, chickens they snatched, and hand-outs from the rejoicing peasants.

M. and Mme Guérigny were glad to be left on their own, to get to know one another again after four years of separation, and to decide what was best to do for the future. They would abandon their slow-thinking community miles from the highway. They would move to the outskirts of Paris. They would buy and sell vegetables. They knew about vegetables, and fruit. They had raised them for generations. Mme Guérigny's brothers had done quite well for themselves not far from Paris, and she, too, wanted to acquire a better standard of living, and some sort of training, possibly, for the two young people. With the help of her brothers and their wives, the Guérignys found the *pavillon*, which they rented for themselves, and for the equivalent of another five pounds a year, the attic of the proprietor's own house for Montaine and Jean-Claude.

While Montaine endured a typing school above the drycleaners in Reine les Falaises, Jean-Claude worked on the attic to make it habitable. No one had much money. The Guérigny parents started in a very small way, unable at first to buy at Les Halles all that their customers in Reine would have liked for their tables. Jean-Claude got accustomed in these early days to stealing. I think he lived off what he stole until he met Otto. Then Otto provided . . . Whatever the case, the habit became ingrained in him. (Otto once told me some unbelievably shocking – to me – tales about Jean-Claude and American soldiers, and how they paid him in cigarettes and chewing-gum. He said that during the war things like that happened.) When I went to live in the attic, Jean-Claude still

74

took it for granted that the wood he needed for the stove should be filched from the railway sidings. 'But it must belong to *someone*,' I argued.

Montaine and Jean-Claude inherited their love of music from their mother. It was essential to their lives, not a luxury. They sang together, played by ear on the old upright that someone from the big house had thrown out and they had retrieved. While they lived in la Sologne it never occurred to either of them that it was even possible for people like themselves to study music and become professional musicians. They made music for the love of it. It was as natural to them as to the birds.

Both kept diaries. Jean-Claude's was in notes, not words. No one else knew of these records, they were just another among the many secrets the two shared. It was only when Jean-Claude came to Paris and was settled in the attic, wondering what to do with the rest of his life, that he realized he was already a composer and the rest of his life would be spent composing. The fact that such an occupation was unlikely to provide him with a living did nothing to deter him.

Meeting Otto was the turning-point. I never knew where Jean-Claude met him or how. When I came into his life he had known Otto for about four years. Montaine was still living in the attic at the time. I remember Otto mentioning that she entertained him there with Jean-Claude, and only later moved out into a room over the Café du Coin, to be nearer her 'young man'. One might imagine that Jean-Claude would have done all he could to dissuade Montaine from decamping. It was not the case. He always spoke as if he was satisfied that she should have a life of her own. Anyhow, there was not space for the two of them in the attic for ever. I got the impression that Jean-Claude had been so certain that his relationship with his sister was the most singular she would ever make, that the mere fact of their not living under the same roof would do nothing to erode what they had together. But I also had the sense that Otto had something to do with Jean-Claude's need for greater privacy.

It was through an introduction made by Otto that Jean-Claude had a composition performed at the Club d'Essai. It was a sonata for piano, dedicated to Montaine, entitled 'La Solognate'. He chose not to perform the piece himself. It was a sensible decision and he may have taken it in full awareness of this. A celebrated pianist gave the performance, and her reputation drew in the public – and the critics. The response was almost unanimous. A new star had shot into the musical firmament.

Otto brought a certain M. Chaillot from French radio to the recital. M. Chaillot had in mind a production of a contemporary translation of *Twelfth Night*. He was on the look-out for someone to write the incidental music, someone with fresh ideas, preferably someone not too well known. He commissioned Jean-Claude.

I saw the score. It was headed with the oddly prophetic 'But died thy sister for her love, my boy?' I read some of the reviews Jean-Claude had slipped into the score. 'Guérigny' was particularly congratulated for his ability to suggest seriousness in levity and levity in seriousness. Critics wrote of the leit-motif for Malvolio that it 'captured the colour mustard', and that Guérigny was 'positively acrobatic in his ability to turn little themes on their heads and send them spinning out of hearing'. One wrote of a passage seeming quite serious and thoughtful, 'cleverly interrupted by the merest hint of a titter'. Through each review Jean-Claude had struck a thick black pencil-line on which he had scrawled *merde*.

I listened to a repeat of the play. I was dazzled by the clarity of Jean-Claude's music. It spoke as mellifluously as the actors spoke their lines. I had 'done' *Twelfth Night* at school and had never thought of music for it. Living in close intimacy with Jean-Claude had not prepared me for confronting in musical shape the qualities I sensed and loved in him but could not define.

Jean-Claude raised the subject of a piano again. This time he did not mention giving lessons but said it would be lovely to be able to play to me. He had seen one advertised, a small upright Bosendorfer. I was not earning nearly enough for a piano, however modestly priced, but it would cost less than I could raise from one of the *famille rose* vases I had brought from the house in Park Terrace. With what was left over we could pay to have it delivered.

It was rare for us to go into the city together. For one thing, a visit always involved spending money on food and drink. For another, Jean-Claude hated taking time off from his work. He composed obsessionally. And so the day we bought the piano was memorable for many reasons. However, whereas it should have been a joyous occasion, it was not. It turned out to be an irritating, sad day.

We rode into the Place St Michel and sat in a café drinking hot chocolate. From the window we could see to the right a barrel-organ with a small dog dressed as a clown, to the left a pile of rags heaped on the Metro ventilation grille. I wondered who had abandoned them there and why they had not been removed. While a small crowd collected around the barrel-organ, a policeman idled across to the pile of rags, thrust his boot into it and said something inaudible. Gradually, the pile heaved and took form, and an old man, dirty and complaining, shuffled off.

'They're quite content with their lives,' Jean-Claude insisted in response to my concern. 'They spend the day sleeping, or rummaging in dust-bins, scraping a living from the debris of the rich.' I could not detect from his tone what Jean-Claude felt about what he was saying. It seemed to me he was not so much indifferent as hostile towards these poor men. He told me, rather as a guide to the city might have recounted it, that before the war there had been flop-houses just to the right of where we were sitting. Tramps slept there *à la corde*, standing, their arms hooked over a rope slung from the corners of the room. He said that the men we saw emerging from the rue de la Huchette into the Place St Michel were probably superannuated rag-pickers. I knew, given the atmosphere Jean-Claude was creating, that it would be better if I did not wonder aloud why, in a civilized country like France, the poor were not looked after better.

The dealer in oriental antiquities worked from home in the Marais. I suggested we park the motor cycle and walk from the Place des Vosges. I wanted to savour the differences this area had to offer. There were French, Arab and Jewish streets; as I passed from one to another I felt I was crossing borders. Jean-Claude's expression soured in the presence of Jewish men in black alpaca coats down to their ankles, and wide-brimmed black hats garnished with fur, from which long twists of black hair hung in curls. These men were scurrying like ants between the kosher butchers, the ritual baths and the tiny, one-room synagogues open to the street. They avoided our glances as if we might bestow the evil eye. I noticed there were no women with them. Perhaps they were cloistered at home or in one of the wig shops. Jean-Claude hurried me along, his expression sweetening when we crossed into the Arab streets. He smiled at the huddles of aimless, olive-skinned men standing outside the couscous bars. While mournful music poured out from loud-speakers, Jean-Claude hummed. The men were gratified and returned his greeting, but stared at me with a mixture of impudence and hostility. It was as if they were taking off my clothes, garment by garment, and did not much appreciate what they saw.

'These are the streets I like, where rough men congregate. I like their bars, their dance-halls, their music. I admire their insolence and brashness, their excesses, their lack of selfconsciousness. There's something honest in all this. But the Jews . . . UGH! They're furtive and disgusting.' And he went on to tell me admiringly how in the Arab quarter the policemen walk in pairs. 'There are deadly feuds! Knives are flashed and revolvers cocked.'

I simply listened. I did not comment. I thought how Father would have spoken out. But I took his arm, and smiled.

M. Lévy's premises stood at the intersection of the Arab and Jewish streets, an ideal situation for his particular trade. He offered Jean-Claude less for the vase than Jean-Claude believed it must be worth.

'Surely Helmut would not have offered you such a trifle!' And turning to M. Lévy: 'This woman's husband is an extremely rich man, he doesn't invest in baubles.' In one sentence Jean-Claude was trying to impress M. Lévy and insult my husband. I felt uncomfortable, and noticed that M. Lévy looked at me sympathetically. 'Take it or leave it!' he said, shrugging his shoulders and turning his back. 'Another late *famille rose* vase, another Bukharan rug – what's it to me?'

I felt uneasy and exposed as we emerged into the street and I watched Jean-Claude pack the money into his inside pocket. Then I heard him mutter to himself: '*Avare comme tous les juifs*'. In Father's house, the term 'Jew' had been an honourable title.

We went to eat lunch in a restaurant frequented by poorly paid clerks and secretaries and, no doubt, messengers. Although I found the food unappetizing, I warmed to the atmosphere of the place. Most of those eating were regulars. Their napkins were kept for them in specially designed pigeon-holes to which they homed on entering, before heading for their tables. The *serveuses* reminded me of those I had seen in paintings by Monet. However, I imagined their less well-corseted flesh was held in place by elastic rather than whalebone, for their fat slipped like butter as they squeezed between the tables and chairs. Jean-Claude concentrated on his food – a leek *vinaigrette*, *steak-frites* and a *flan*. 'One knows what one's getting with a *steak-frites* . . .' But when he had finished eating he seemed to want it known that he was not of the company. He rose to his full height and surveyed the scene with his chin too high and his eyes half closed, peering, as if what he viewed was rather beneath his dignity. 'Come,' he said, clicking his fingers at one of the *serveuses*, 'when I finally succeed in getting the bill out of someone, I'll take you to Père Lachaise.'

The trees grow tall, but their new leaves quickly turn sooty and diseased at the cemetery of Père Lachaise. The monuments are grotesque; each reflects the worst aspects of the taste of its time. Were the wishes of those they commemorate taken into consideration? I wondered, as I followed Jean-Claude along the gravel paths between the *arrondissements* of the dead. How little I tolerate marble, in whatever colour; it is so cold. Grey granite, cement, no better. Nor dirty white wax. These are the colours and materials of death's craftsmen. In the twilight groves and dusty caves there is no sign of what it is to be alive: nothing of love, valour or artistry. I suppose the presence of such qualities would be considered in bad taste.

At first, I was surprised that Jean-Claude praised mournful Père Lachaise for being mournful: just that. But as I watched him pick his way along the lifeless paths, I understood how much of him expected the whole world to be mournful now that Montaine had abandoned it. Death is a member of the Guérigny family. I was trying hard to adjust to this fact but finding it difficult. In Père Lachaise all was properly harrowing. Jean-Claude told me that is was here he had wished Montaine to be laid, not in the familiar old churchyard within a stone's throw of the house. In Père Lachaise the dead were disturbed only on anniversaries. In Reine they were apt to be intruded upon weekly. Many mourners at Père Lachaise made their pilgrimages once in a lifetime – and left eternally inert blooms, the insignia of melancholy. Mourners at Reine left pretty little bouquets of daisies and roses.

'They have no sense of occasion. They fail to observe the right of the dead to be left in peace. Montaine *chose* peace. What more can the dead ask than to have this wish granted? Who wants the weekly, self-pitying tears of the living? My God! Is it not enough to have to endure that when one is alive?'

It was in this frame of mind that Jean-Claude took me with him to view the piano.

I met Helmut for lunch at Fouquet's. He was already seated, waiting to order. He rose, but did not kiss me. When I was settled at his side he turned to scrutinize me. He remarked that I looked neither well nor happy.

'Are you happy?'

'Very.'

'You eat like a sparrow,' he said, when I declined more than nine oysters. I seemed to have nothing to say to him and was glad he talked about his business. When he started to inquire about my life, I deflected the conversation by saying that I had sold one of the *famille* rose vases.

'My dear child, how many times can I have told you never to split a pair! Of anything. A pair of anything is worth at least seventy per cent more than two identical items sold singly.'

'Please don't be cross.' I think I was feeling guilty although we must have been equally relieved to have the subject at our disposal.

'I am not cross. I gave you the vases as a present for your room, and you are perfectly at liberty to dispose of them as and when you see fit. It's just that you would have raised much more if you'd sold the pair. Or perhaps you wanted to hold on to one for sentimental reasons?' I turned to look at him. Was he being sarcastic? Anyhow, I could not lie. 'And how much did you get for the one?' I told him. 'Oh dear! Tell me, what was the name of this particular thief?' Helmut had not heard of M. Lévy. He said that if in future I needed to sell oriental porcelain I should go to M. Bourget, in the rue de Berri, and mention Helmut's name. 'Did you need the money urgently?' He sounded concerned. I told him Jean-Claude needed a piano. 'Ah . . . ah,' he murmured. I had the impression that Helmut no longer liked me much. He seemed in a hurry to get away to his next appointment.

When I got back to the attic, I was surprised to find Jean-Claude was not alone. He was sitting talking to a middle-aged, bearded man dressed in a curiously outdated suit which he was wearing shirtless, over a vest. On his feet he had faded, worn espadrilles.

'Félix is *interdit de séjour*.' I noticed the man's stained fingers had warts. His nails were bitten to the quick. 'He's forbidden to visit Paris at all, let alone stay overnight. We're going to put him up for a few days. But because we mustn't let anyone know he's here, there are a few precautions we must take. Don't buy for three in any of the shops. Go to Roules for our usual meat but buy the third chop down at Blance's.' I looked at Jean-Claude as he gave me these instructions and I saw a side of him I did not recognize. He put his arm round me but I did not want to be caressed.

I was never to discover for what misdemeanour Félix Vaugirard had been penalized. I knew better than to inquire. All I knew about him was that he was someone who belonged to Jean-Claude's past, and that Jean-Claude was indebted to him. He asked me for 50,000 francs for Félix. I would have to sell the second vase.

Félix wandered round the attic peering into books and papers – and even jars in the kitchen. He was restless and anxious and drank coffee non-stop. He was particularly put out by the absence of a telephone. He had calls to make. He would solve the problem of the lack of a lavatory by using a bucket in the unused part of the attic. He must on no account be seen by the neighbours. He told me to buy him cigarettes and stamps when I went out to the shops. He did not give me the money for either.

He ate pork chops in tomato sauce with us that evening, and claimed it was the first good meal he had had in six months. He had been hiding out, sleeping rough, until three days ago when he arrived in Paris to look up another man indebted to him. This man allowed him to wash, and sleep for forty-eight hours, and gave him a cast-off, vintage suit, but then turned him out. He had every intention of getting the hell out of Paris just as soon as he had collected all the money owed to him. I wondered how it had happened that so many men owed Félix money. For one thing, he did not look the sort from whom one would borrow. He did not look as if he had ever had much to lend. But I could have been wrong and I had no means of checking my suspicions.

'Just go back to Lévy tomorrow and sell the other vase,' Jean-Claude told me rather conspiratorially when Félix had gone to his bucket. 'He'll leave as soon as I pay him off.' The way Jean-Claude was speaking made me anxious. 'Pay him off': what did that imply? I could imagine only blackmail.

Jean-Claude fetched a mattress from the *pavillon* and laid it in his working space. Although Félix slept more soundly than we did – and snored and swore in his sleep – for the three nights he stayed, Jean-Claude and I could not feel comfortable about making love. And I noticed another thing:

Jean-Claude was tetchy. He said it was because he could not work with Félix around. But he was offhand with me and seemed to be waiting all the time for me to go out. It was I who was made to feel the intruder.

The Métro was very crowded. I left Reine early, when all the people who live on the outskirts of Paris pour in to the city to work. I had wrapped the vase carefully in newspaper and put it in a string bag, which I slung over my shoulder. I was glad to get a seat. To while away the time and take my mind off Félix, I read the names of the Métro stations off the chart on the carriage wall: Danube, Bolivar, Rome, Bir Hakeim, Jasmin . . . Each name brought to mind wonderful associations, incomparable possibilities for the future. I would visit each of these locations – in time. I believe it was on this ride that I sensed something I had not felt since the time I took my French classes in London: a sort of exhilarating separateness. I was rediscovering that impenetrable area of existence that was safe from intruders.

M. Lévy gave me a third more for the second vase than he had given Jean-Claude for the first one. He said he could tell I needed the money. I could have kissed him.

I was alone. The day was mine. Jean-Claude would be pleased with me for staying out of the attic. I would go to the Marché aux Puces. I had heard Jean-Claude say that everything was cheap there, and I needed things for the attic. I had never visited a huge, second-hand market before. Where I had come from, in the English provinces, the markets were quite small, and reserved for food. There would be one or two stalls selling bits of radios, farm machinery and so on, but I had never felt inclined to rummage in them. At Les Puces there was everything that everyone had ever thrown out: genuine, valuable antiques, odd shoes, false teeth, stuffed cats . . . more items than I knew existed. Several times I was stopped in my tracks by the sight of something I could not identify. I did not like to ask the dealers questions. They looked a dangerous lot.

There was a little shop in my home town that I had liked very much, selling old bits and pieces, books and engravings; all that was for sale was in a jumble, and the windows had not been cleaned in years. The owner always stayed at the back with his mongrel at his feet, unless one called him out, and paid no attention to potential customers. But shopping in Les Puces was still more to my taste. There was no bell to sound my coming or going, no wearing out of someone else's carpet and electricity; no animal to be disturbed from sleep. I could examine what I wanted to examine, pick it up, smell it, read the books, flip over the cards, listen to gramophone records on a wind-up machine with a huge convolvulus-shaped horn. I could even try on old clothes. And I was never at risk of being spoken to or of having to endure sales talk. I forgot Félix. I forgot that someone was living illegally in Paris on the floor of my home and demanding a large sum of money to leave.

I bought some lovely old half-glazed pots, two plates and a jug – not matching, but probably from the same pottery in the Midi. I found some cotton stuff that would do nicely to replace the sacking at our windows, and a pair of linen sheets. I felt a little ashamed of these purchases. I had bought them for very little money from a woman who looked needy. I wondered whether it was right to take the items from her.

The Spartan asceticism in the attic as I had first experienced it was giving way to small comforts. I was even planning to find a little electric water-heater to put over the sink. It was not that I objected to the public baths. It was just that it would make life a little easier.

The baths were quite an important part of my life in Reine. They were situated beyond the Café du Coin. To the left of the café, the rue Sèvres ended in a waste-land where pigs were kept. To the right, the rue Foch drove straight to the Métro at the *Porte*. The baths stood a hundred yards down the rue Foch, past the *Mairie*, the printing works and *la maison du sauvage*, where a hermit lived in a courtyard barricaded with oil drums and fastened with chains and umpteen locks.

I liked the walk to the baths. I was fascinated by all I saw on my way. I went mid-week in the afternoon, when the streets were filled with activity and the baths were empty. I became friendly with the woman in charge, a vast and haughty person who answered to the sobriquet *Duchesse*. She liked the title; she felt grand in a grand house. She would have made an excellent Madame.

The routine was to enter and pay one franc for the bath. The money went, I think, to the local authority. But if one required a towel and soap, the *Duchesse* provided both and the money went into the pocket of her apron. I availed myself of this service. I realized she relied on the extra money. The custom was then to take a seat in the steam-filled lobby, by her table and chair ('desk' would be to exaggerate), while she prepared a cubicle. Making this ready might involve cleaning it after a previous bather and then running fresh water. When the water reached a level the *Duchesse* deemed suffficient (she was mean with it with people she did not like), she called out for the bather to come along, and she left, taking the handle of the hot tap with her. This she confined to the pocket in her overall. When a bather wanted more hot water, he or she had to shout over the noise of filling baths and protesting bathers and the *Duchesse* singing, and depending on how this eccentric woman felt, she would either top up the water from a source outside the cubicles or tell the bather his time was up. She grumbled to me that if she left the tap-handles *in situ*, people would take advantage and lie in their baths for hours on end, using a lot more hot water than their franc entitled them to. '*C'est défendu!*' she uttered repeatedly, with all the authority of a park-keeper waving a child off the grass.

As I made my way back to the Métro I felt a sort of heightened awareness. I revelled in the capricious vegetation wrought in iron – even the sound of water running in the urinals was pleasing. I found myself humming to the tune of the violin an old man was playing for sous. I would have liked to drink coffee in one of the smoke-filled cafés lining the boulevard, but I did not dare enter. In each place a crowd of men in blue overalls, each with a Gauloise stuck in the corner of his mouth, stared into the mirror behind the bar at the reflection of any women who braved their domain. I was not up to such men. I can remember wondering whether I ever would be.

It was when he was commissioned to write seventeen and a half minutes of light music for the radio that I discovered why Jean-Claude had insisted I bring from London some of my most beautifully tailored suits and expensive dresses. Whether he had had plans laid for me at the time, or whether at the back of his mind, hidden from consciousness, he knew that in taking me to live with him he would be enrolling someone to deal with the business side of his life, I was never sure. Whatever the case, I slipped into that role quickly, glad to be useful. There was some truth in Jean-Claude's assertion that rich and powerful men are apt to take advantage of poor, uninfluential ones. And he may well have been correct in thinking that, in France at any rate, such men were less likely to take advantage of women. They liked women, after all. What he told me was that M. Chaillot adored the company of women and would wish to charm me. He picked out a Hardy Amies suit and blouse for me to wear – and masses of Helmut's jewels pinned to the suit, fastened to my ears and draped round my neck. 'There!' he said, stepping back to examine me, 'he won't dare insult you.'

Jean-Claude made the appointment for six o'clock at M. Chaillot's *appartement* in Passy. M. Chaillot was the commissioning director of the music pro-gramme at Radio Française. He had a reputation for finding the best and paying the least. I was so anxious not to be late for my appointment that I got to Passy two hours early. It was a glorious day, so I did not mind. I explored.

If Helmut had lived in Paris, he would have chosen Passy, I am sure of that. He liked private places behind high walls, and there were lots of houses like that, with gardens, where M. Chaillot lived. And Helmut liked to feel he was stepping in the footprints of celebrated men. M. Chaillot was proud to be living close to Balzac's house. The equivalent of the high street in Passy was much smarter than anything I had seen in London. There were shops solely devoted to hand-made choco-lates, sold in boxes quilted like cushions. And in the windows of the *pâtisserie,* where the cakes were little works of art in their own right, I counted a dozen three-foot bottles of *marrons* in cognac. Next to the butcher, where the meat was arranged on silver platters and the chops dressed with paper ruffs, I saw for the first time a shop stocked exclusively with cheeses: nothing else, just cheese. There must have been five hundred varieties. I entered. The smell was a little overpowering. A man in a spotless white coat offered me little pieces of cheese to taste from the end of a special curved knife. The interior of the shop was beautiful. It was kept cool for the sake of the product, and the décor itself was cool. There was a blue-and-white frieze of cows and sheep and goats right round the shop, at eye-level. And there was a picture engraved on glass, illustrating the fable of the milkmaid and her pail. I explained to the man that I could not carry cheese to my appointment but that I would be back another day. I went to sit in the Pâtisserie Louis, on a fragile gilt chair, at a table with a pink linen cloth and a bowl of freesias. I pondered: the war had ravaged France, the Germans had overrun Paris, how was it that the people had recovered so quickly? Why, in England, where there had been no invasion, did we drink watery coffee, eat cakes made with margarine, in dirty cafés decorated with ivy and bamboo wallpaper?

Walking from the café and the food shops, I passed two ostentatious jewellers. What sort of woman, I asked myself, drops into a jeweller's for a brooch costing thousands of francs, between buying a gigot and a gâteau St Honoré? Olga, perhaps. Yes, if Olga lived in Paris, she too would almost certainly choose Passy.

Jean-Claude must have told M. Chaillot that, because of a bereavement, he was not up to contracts and their clauses, and discussions relating to money. (Otto had evidently coped for him in the past.) M. Chaillot quickly expressed his regret that Jean-Claude should be grieving. I could not think quite what to say and murmured something unintelligible. Would I take a seat? Did I smoke? Would I like to take a turn round the garden? The English do so love gardens! Empty conviviality, set like a trap.

'Jean-Claude, you understand, is not celebrated. However, he is collecting a small, faithful following. You must be reasonable, my dear young lady. A young man can live on love and spring water, *n'est-ce pas?* The Radio Française is a public corporation. We are entrusted with public funds. Jean-Claude must not encourage you to become over-demanding on his account.'

I understood only too well why Jean-Claude chose not to deal with M. Chaillot himself. But I did wonder whether he knew quite how keen M. Chaillot was on young women.

'The British are the only women who know how to wear tweeds,' he said, looking me up and down. 'These lightweight, cobweb stuffs are exquisite. I let my wife buy Harris and Cheviot lengths for winter when she's in London, but I never allow her to have them made up for herself. She's away for a few days. She will be so sorry to have missed you.' M. Chaillot was by now unexpectedly by my side, opening a huge satin-covered box of chocolates of the cream-filled variety I had seen in the local shop. 'It's so much more sensible for the artist to have an agent to deal with contracts. Artists are terribly difficult people for us ordinary mortals to deal with. Hopeless with money . . . I know, you'll ask where would we all be without them?' And he lit a cigar. 'But where would we be without the farmer and the bus-driver? *They* don't make demands on us, do they?' I declined a chocolate; they were too large to take in in one bite and I feared to take two and risk cream and liqueur trickling down my chin. 'A drink, perhaps?' And M. Chaillot arranged himself in front of an eighteenth-century writing-table, lacquered with green *vernis Martin*. Each of the legs of the table incorporated a naked ormolu caryatid. Before he poured me a drink M. Chaillot stood puffing his cigar and fondling the breasts of one of the figures. I was made nervous, but was careful not to seem so.

Looking back, I cannot imagine that I understood the finer points of the contract M. Chaillot placed before me. I had seen only one other signed by Jean-Claude before. I vowed I would do better for him, but no doubt overlooked some of the conditions relating to repeat performances and foreign rights. All my attention focused on the commissioning fee, which I regarded as derisory. I said so; Émile Chaillot raised no objection to the sum I suggested would be more appropriate. On the contrary, he looked at me admiringly, flourished his pen, wrote in the sum, turned the page, signed and asked me to do likewise on Jean-Claude's account. 'That seems a great deal of money to me!' But he was trying me out. One has to be rich, I thought, to exaggerate the charms of small sums.

The deal I concluded for Jean-Claude amounted to twice the sum that had been pencilled in. No doubt M. Chaillot agreed to my demand only because he imagined I would regard his acceptance of it as an incentive to call again.

'It's so much more congenial to meet here than in my office at the radio.'

He was paving the way to amusing himself with me in the future when Mme Chaillot was out of town. But I was braced to cope with him because I had been ambitious for Jean-Claude, vaunt-ingly so. At last my boyish figure had acquired some status and a more attractive description: *gamine*. My barren womb, once so degrading, had become a positive qualification, giving me the opportunity of generating money in place of babies. I was in no doubt that my lover had talent, but I had no doubt, too, that he would have remained either in relative obscurity or at the mercy of the likes of M. Chaillot and others had he not come across me.

The piano that we had inspected and paid for in the city was delivered by three young Arabs in a beat-up van. Jean-Claude helped the men up our four flights of stairs with their cumbersome delivery and, having given them beer, rewarded them with a generous tip. He evidently knew one of them. I heard him say *à bientôt* to him, and saw him run his hand gently over the man's arm. An unidentifiable feeling shot through me.

We agreed that the piano should not be put in our part of the attic. It would take up more space than we could spare. The solution was to take over some of the unconverted part of the attic. It would be quite an easy job; it only involved erecting another partition, cleaning the floorboards and reglazing the window. Jean-Claude liked this sort of activity. It occupied him without posing intractable problems. Not like composing. He said he was glad to have the third view. He could already see over the rue Victorie at the front and over his father's garden at the back. Now he could see to the lane that led to the *pavillon*.

The piano was an intrusion. I could feel the strong arm of Montaine's custody of Jean-Claude when he played. He became stingy with words, and sombre. I was finding him unreachable – except in bed. He dreamed often of his sister. And every morning after such a dream, she died again for him. He told me that before I had come to live with him he never listened to the radio for fear of hearing a song she had liked to sing or a piece of piano music she used to play. One day when we were sitting reading together, the couple in the room below the attic let their radio blare. Faure's *Adieu* enveloped us. I watched Jean-Claude grapple unsuccessfully with a knife at his heart.

Within weeks, however, I felt a change in Jean-Claude's mood: he was happier and more present to me. We had been reading the poems of a Greek poet in French translation together. Each of the poems looked at a different sort of love: that of parents and children, of friends, of lovers, of God . . . We discussed the idea of Jean-Claude setting them to piano accompaniment. What did I think of his idea of linking the poems with short passages elaborating and co-ordinating the motifs of the poem before and the one to follow? He discussed every detail of the cycle with me while he composed for it. He made me feel that my ideas and my interest were important to him. He was hugely enthusiastic about this work and telephoned M. Chaillot, who said he was interested in principle but would need a little time to think about it. Jean-Claude sang him one of the poems over the telephone. M. Chaillot's response included the information that there was not much money for new work in his budget. He had spent too much on——, and he mentioned Jean-Claude's *bête noire*. A composer with all the right connections . . . Jean-Claude repeated to me every detail of the conversation and the argument that ensued. I told him proudly he should never in future discuss money in relation to his work. That was my job now. We kissed. We were happy. Jean-Claude said I was invaluable.

He was a martyr to fatigue. Mme Guérigny once told me that Jean-Claude's weakness was in part due to his exemplary sensitivity and in part to the damp in the cave, which had affected his lungs and his joints. Seizing on all impending illnesses with enthusiasm, she emphasized the usefulness of herbal infusions. She also provided some herbal oil with which I was to massage Jean-Claude's limbs. Mme Guérigny was obsessed by matters relating to health – pharmaceutically rather than compassionately. She had raised Jean-Claude, she was intimate with his variety of complaints, she knew their origins, and there were remedies. The only occasions upon which she came into the attic herself were pharmaceutically driven, to bring tablets, linctus, suppositories, or to 'cup' her son. Cupping was new to me. It involved thrusting a lighted taper into little glass jars and applying them in great haste to Jean-Claude's back, which would bubble up under them in balloons of skin. The evidence of this remedy lasted for weeks in circular scars from his shoulders to his waist. Mme

Guérigny insisted that I watch closely while she performed this rite. It would save her poor feet if she did not have to mount the stairs to the attic. Had she insisted that I apply leeches to her son I could not have felt more disturbed, more unwilling to assist at this medieval rite. As prescribed by Mme Guérigny, French cures were altogether different from English ones – and many, if not most, were administered at the back rather than the front end.

I was not used to patients. Mother had been taken ill suddenly and at once removed to hospital, where she died within a few days. Father was never ill. I cannot remember his taking a single day in bed. He said he did not have the time. Helmut was the same. In Reine les Falaises I encountered more ill-health and death than ever before. Precautions had to be taken on a daily basis: draughts were mortal; the liver constantly under threat. If Jean-Claude sneezed, it was not the sign of an oncoming cold but of flu. And flu led to pneumonia. If he had an upset stomach, it was not something he had eaten, indigestion, but the first sign of a rumbling ulcer. A bruised rib was taken for heart trouble, a headache for an incipient brain tumor. When he insisted he needed a holiday, I agreed that it would be lovely to lie in the sun and swim in the warm Mediterranean, but I could not agree that it was an urgent need. I suggested that, in any case, it might be wise to postpone going away until we had heard from M. Chaillot regarding the 'Chansons de Mani'.

'Otto has invited us to Les Glycines.'

'Where is that?'

'In the Midi.'

Otto's invitation, Jean-Claude said, could not wait on M. Chaillot's decision. Otto was a busy man, he could not take time off when he wanted. We were privileged to have been invited . . . one doesn't make difficulties . . . I could see all that.

France raced under our two wheels. Paris was behind us, and with it Mme Guérigny's Sunday lunches, Félix, clandestine telephone conversations, and the plundering of my belongings. We made the journey in three days; we could have done it in two but we chose not to. We stopped the first night at an inn on the banks of a river. We were served trout plucked from the river specially for us, under an awning on a wooden balcony overhanging the water. We could barely hear one another speak above the sound of the nearby mill-race. We spent our second night in a fortified hill village. We lodged with the proprietor of the Café de la Place. There was no inn as such. I felt I had stepped back into a thirties' film and that in the morning, when we went down into the bar for *café au lait*, Arletty and Jean Gabin would be leaning on the zinc counter.

We were very happy. We were carefree. Jean-Claude had all the music worked out for the 'Chansons', there was nothing to worry about there, and something good to come home to.

101

Riding through the French countryside burgeoning with corn, barley, vines, fruit and vegetables, I felt not only replete myself but part of plenty.

Otto's house stood in the middle of vineyards. We arrived by the light of the moon. Had Jean-Claude not known the way we should undoubtedly have got lost. The house hung to the side of terracing. From it one could see lights twinkling in the little town below, and fishing-boats with lights at sea. But the road that ran from the town, called Théovard, bypassed Les Glycines five hundred yards to the north, and we dismounted rather than run the motor cycle over the pitted lane.

Although it was very late, Otto whisked us off to dine that night at a restaurant some way along the coast. It must have been eleven o'clock by the time we sat down to eat. The place was crowded, filled with bronzed men in pale linen suits and bronzed women in backless silk dresses, with heady scents and masses of gold jewellery.

I woke early next morning, roused by the creaking of the cicadas and the scent of orange blossom. Jean-Claude, exhausted by the long ride from Paris and a late night of intoxication, moaned something unintelligible as I got out of bed, rolled over and promptly went back to sleep. Otto had been true to his word and left out for me a pair of boy's shorts. I did not own such a garment; I had stopped wearing shorts when I left school, determined never again to be taken for a 'lad'. When I put my hands in the pockets I felt banknotes. I was sure Otto had put them there for me.

At dinner he had spoken about the market in the Place Mistral. He said that if I woke early – and most visitors from Paris did wake early their first few mornings – I should get up straightaway and walk into town.

'It won't take you more than twenty-five minutes. It's downhill all the way.' And he counselled me to take note of the sea. 'It's at its bluest early. Later it turns slightly green.'

It was six o'clock when I let myself out of the house. I took the path through the vegetable garden, between the serried rows of artichokes and onions. And where this path ended, at the hedge of rosemary bushes, I walked along the edge of the vineyard where the vines, their branches outstretched to one another, appeared frozen in a formal dance. I came upon a very old woman dressed from hat to woollen stockings and high boots in black. She was bending over a basket of freshly picked marrow flowers, arranging them to her satisfaction. A rush-seated wooden chair stood by the well, in the shade of a fig tree. I murmured *bonjour* but she did not hear. She seemed not to notice me.

The sun was pale over the mountains. There was not the merest breeze. I felt an almost unbearably painful sense of beauty and order – painful because

I could not imagine it would prevail. I looked behind me. Otto's house was now concealed from view behind groves of sombre cypresses. All was fixed, still. Neither man nor beast was abroad. I walked on to the sea's edge. I sat down on a rock in the golden air and stared at the vast expanse of glassy blue and listened to the sucking and lapping. I thought I had found paradise.

The narrow street that led into the town was lined with tall, thin houses painted pale fruit colours – apricot, raspberry and greengage. Each had a balcony at first-floor level on which geraniums bloomed in old tins. I was being drawn into the centre of the town by the sound of a church bell throbbing. As I approached I heard shop shutters shooting up, greetings being exchanged, children and dogs being admonished. Where the street broadened into a square, the houses were swathed in plumbago and bougainvillaea growing valiantly out of the cobbled pavement.

I chose a café overlooking the port. The fishing-boats groaned as the men lugged their catch on to the promenade. The sun was up. So, too, was the entire population of Théovard-sur-Mer.

Théovard has two hearts: the port, and the market in the Place Mistral. The men fish and sell their catch along the little promenade. The women grow fruit, vegetables and flowers, and raise flesh to sell in the Place Mistral. Both occupations gave rise to perpetual celebration. It was as if a harvest festival were enacted daily, for throughout the hours of market the church bell tolled quietly. It seemed not to seek to impose itself but merely to mark the occasion. Was this celebration, six years after the Liberation, a reminder of less happy times? The bell did nothing to drown the sound of anxious hens and ducks. I wondered if it was responsible for the quiet acceptance of their fate shown by the rabbits chewing their final greenery. There were women hidden behind piles of blood-red peppers, royal purple aubergines, curdwhite cauliflowers and spinach green as envy. There were shallow baskets lined with grasses stacked with ducks', hens' and gulls' eggs – white, brown and blue. There were flat baskets, almost trays, with cheeses, white, yellow and brown, dressed in vine leaves, straw and muslin, the produce of goats, ewes and cows. In small, nicely made wooden drums there were new potatoes no larger than damsons. And in galvanized buckets all sorts of olives – large, small, smooth, wrinkled, black and green, dressed with pistachios and almonds, herbs, spices, garlic, lemon and oil. There were sausages strung like fat paperchains between stalls. The women who sat beside a single basket of herbs, or wild mushrooms they had gathered that morning in the dew, high in the hills, were tanned so dark they might have washed in walnut juice.

Before tearing myself away, I stopped at the edge of the market beside the asparagus-seller. Whereas all else had been a matter of pleasantries, he was ribald. Holding high small thin green shoots thicker than a matchstick but no thicker than a pencil, he jeered at women satisfied, he said, by 'little boys'. He reached for a bunch of thick white stalks with plump purple bulbs. 'Which of you can take on men?' he sniggered.

I wandered into the church. It was a simple, ancient place, and above all I welcomed the cool. I was tired. I decided to take the road back to Les Glycines. It would be a less beautiful route than the one I had taken earlier, but it was shorter and would be less of a haul.

It was some time after ten o'clock that I strolled through the gate on to the terrace. I took stock of the bees in the wisteria and the cat stretching itself under the table. I noticed that the front door was open, as I had left it. I was uncomfortably hot. I would shower and change into a dress. I was longing to describe to Jean-Claude all I had seen. There was a palpable silence in the house. Jean-Claude must still be sleeping. Perhaps Otto was out. I moved quietly towards our bedroom. As I approached the bead curtain that hung in place of a door, I was aware of movement behind the strands of wood beads, a rhythmical rising and falling, murmuring, sighing. I stepped back, holding my breath. I could not identify my feelings, they must have been those of shock. My stomach was churning. I was going to be sick. I must be quiet; they must not hear my heart thumping or my involuntary gasp. I slid awkwardly across to the bathroom and hung my head over the lavatory-pan.

When Otto and Jean-Claude joined me on the terrace an hour or so later, they brought iced drinks. Where had I been? Had I found the market? What did I think of Théovard? And where would I most like to spend the rest of the day?

I was feeling winded, as if I had been shot. I was seriously disturbed. I scanned the faces of the two men who, suddenly, seemed strangers. Clearly, nothing between them was amiss. They were behaving affectionately and were joking. They made what seemed to me rather artificial efforts to draw me into the conversation. I had nothing to say. Part of me was anxious for Jean-Claude. Had he been willing for Otto to do what he did? Of course he must have been: Otto would never have acted without Jean-Claude's consent. Ever since they had known one another, Otto had been kindness itself to Jean-Claude. I wondered what I was doing there at Les Glycines.

At the back of my mind lay the knowledge that there were men who enjoyed themselves sexually with other men. It was not, however, a subject I had ever thought about. It was not a matter with which I had been confronted. It worried me that I had reacted as I had. My reaction had been spontaneous and visceral. And then I started to wonder if what I had seen had some connection with the secret telephone calls Jean-Claude made, and the evenings he spent apart from me with nameless friends.

I watched the two closely. I wanted to detect any signs of discomfort. There were none. Both men seemed relaxed. It did not at the time occur to me that their behaviour together had anything to do with what went on between Jean-Claude and me. I did not connect what I had happened upon with love. Indeed it seemed to me that what they were involved in was some sort of violence, and I felt frightened. I could not understand how it was that they were discussing so placidly Jean-Claude's current compositional ideas for the 'Chansons de Mani'. And then Otto went indoors to the piano and played a few bars of Debussy to illustrate a musical idea. No, that was not what Jean-Claude had in mind, and he rose and went inside a played a few bars of something by Scriabin. The two men were alone together indoors and I was on the terrace. My feeling of distaste and fear manifested itself in mounting irritability. I was alone again, and the sound of the piano was invasive – an insult to the peculiar peace in the hills. These men were not only violating my peace of mind but all other sorts of peace. I was preoccupied. I felt a sort of outrage. But it must have been short-lived.

On the surface, at least, our days passed harmoniously, eating, swimming, wandering about in the hills. Jean-Claude enjoyed me at night, and I enjoyed him. There was no lessening of ardour between us. However, if what I had seen take place between him and Otto was to be a habit, I did not want to be a spectator to it. I took myself off for long walks along the shore and into the hills every morning and did not return to Les Glycines until noon, when the three of us would drive in Otto's *traction avant* to one of his favourite places for seafood.

When one day Jean-Claude had to go and find a spare part for the Motobécane which was not obtainable in Théovard, Otto cornered me. He guided me on to the terrace to share a bottle of one of his finest vintages. He started being sickeningly ingratiating, but I felt from the start he was gliding towards insult. He did so hope I was enjoying myself. He did so hope I was not bored with country life. Was this not, however, the most beautiful spot on earth? He went into the kitchen and returned with a plate of local delicacies which he offered me together with a little plate, a napkin and a finger-bowl.

'The English – and of course I don't want you to take this personally – the English are peculiar in that they have very little culinary self-esteem. They are prepared to fashion themselves out of custard, breakfast cereals and boiled cabbage. Why is it – perhaps you can enlighten me – why is it, for example, they roast topside of beef in the first place and in the second cook it to the consistency of baked cow-pat?' And as he spoke he raised a prawn coated with aioli to his lips and took a draught of wine. 'The French, on the other hand, not only insist on a wide variety of fresh produce but demand that their chestnuts come from the Auvergne, their snails from Clermont, their frogs from Aurillac, capons from the Bresse, mutton from the Berry, asparagus from Lavris . . .' On and on he spoke of food. No doubt I had a lot to learn, but this was boring me. Perhaps he noticed, for he stopped and asked me whether Jean-Claude ever spoke of Montaine.

'Never,' I told him.

'Never?' He was surprised.

'Never! Maybe he is getting over his bereavement,' I suggested.

Otto dismissed this possibility. Only the day before, Jean-Claude had told him how, when he visited the room over the café six months after Montaine's suicide, he had smelt her presence. The room was not where she had lived but where she no longer lived. It had been midsummer. The heat in Paris was unbearable, and yet in Montaine's room a peculiar chill persisted. The frozen fingers of death clutched at everything, were curled round every piece of furniture and clawed every drape.

'You are like Montaine,' Otto said. 'You have preserved that innocent expression that belongs to childhood and seldom survives it.' He was regarding me with an indulgence that did not convince me. Without bringing it to the front of my mind, I sensed that Otto felt himself in competition with me, whilst at the same time seeming imperturbable.

He got up and went into the house. I wandered towards the open country and the hills. A wind was gusting from the sea, it clasped small stones and dust, and threw fistfuls at my head. As I retreated, putting one foot down in front of the other on the stony path, I reflected that I was tired of this place, that it had the dry consistency of chaff. When I left the path, thorns penetrated my espadrilles. Looking back, I noticed for the first time how wind-bent and close-cropped were the cypresses. They were all thrown forward in the same direction.

Jean-Claude announced himself rested and refreshed when we got back to Paris. We were both brown and I was glad that we were alone again. We settled into our routine: I walked a dog belonging to a widower who was out at work all day, as well as teaching Didier English; Jean-Claude was working on the 'Chansons de Mani'. His work was going well. I was anxious to settle the terms of the contract with M. Chaillot and, because I wanted to avoid being cornered by him in Passy, I suggested to Jean-Claude that he make an appointment for me to see him at the radio, mid-morning, on a date when I had a luncheon appointment. M. Chaillot fell for the ruse. Perhaps he did not like to argue with Jean-Claude, suspecting that my lover may have been put fully in the picture.

M. Chaillot attempted to drive a hard bargain.

However, I had spoken to Otto on the subject of contracts and was very much better informed since my stay at Les Glycines. I was less moved than ever by M. Chaillot's little lecture on his responsibilities to the public purse. Indeed, I was quite cross and showed it. Calmly, I inquired if he had ever visited Jean-Claude's home. No, he had not. And so I took the opportunity to describe in some detail conditions in the attic. I told him about the cold-water tap, how it did not always produce more than a trickle, how frequently the pressure let us down. I told him about the lavatory on the entrance floor, which did for the fourteen tenants in the house. I told him flatly, and I told him to shock. I believe my success was largely due to the way I looked. I was dressed in a cream linen suit with a light grey silk blouse. I wore high-heeled linen pumps. My legs were nut-brown. My whole presence was utterly out of keeping with what I was describing. I may have reminded him of his wife or daughter. Why, I asked, did he find it acceptable for an artist to have to put up with the paltry sums of money he offered when he himself lived in such style? 'Artists can do without bureaucrats,' I told him. 'Bureaucrats can't do without artists, however.' My words were interrupted by a full measure of 'My dear young lady'. But the contract I agreed to sign on behalf of Jean-Claude was a very different one from the one M. Chaillot had intended me to sign.

As I passed the bakery on my way home, Didier ran out of the shop to greet me and asked if he might accompany me. I laughed and said he might if he spoke English. He told me this and that, but I listened with only half an ear. I was thinking about my conquest. I was proud of myself and hoped Jean-Claude would be proud of me. When I pushed open the gate to the courtyard I was aware of a commotion. Mme Guérigny was standing at the front door, her head pushed back, shouting up to the attic window for Jean-Claude. She was clearly agitated. Spotting me, she screamed for me to go and get Jean-Claude. 'Monsieur Guérigny's had a stroke. The doctor's coming.'

I showed concern and then ran towards the stairs, but Didier stopped me. 'He's not there!' he said.

'Where is he?' I asked.

'I'll show you.'

By this time Mme Guérigny was half-way down the lane to the *pavillon*. I called after her that Jean-Claude was not at home but that I would find him. Didier took my hand and pulled me along the rue Victorie in the direction of the Café du Coin. I wondered, if Jean-Claude were there, why the child had not said so and gone to fetch him for me? But we did not stop at the café. We bore left, and I found we were in the rue de Sèvres.

Didier dropped my hand and ran ahead. I watched him as he bounded up a flight of narrow concrete steps and banged his fists on a shabby door. There was no response from within. Nothing happened. He banged again. I noticed he was too short to reach the bells. He kicked the door several blows. The noise of his boots made the rue de Sèvres sound suspiciously quiet. And then someone threw up a window on the second floor and demanded to know what the hell was going on. 'Can't a woman get a few hours sleep of an afternoon?' the slattern inquired of Didier. And then she saw he was not alone.

'Forgive me for disturbing you,' I said, 'but it's urgent. Someone's ill. Have you seen Monsieur Guérigny?'

'Why should I have seen Monsieur Guérigny?' she asked. 'I'll fetch Mac.' The woman frightened me.

'Who's Mac?' I asked Didier.

'*Le maquereau!*' he answered in French. I had never imagined the usefulness of teaching him English for this particular trade.

A middle-aged man opened the door. He was wearing a shiny black suit and white-and-black golfing shoes, but he was shirtless and sockless. He was chewing on an unlighted cheroot.

'Is Monsieur Guérigny there?' I asked, anxiously adding that his father had been taken ill. If I did not add this information, I felt I should be told that he had never heard of M. Guérigny. I thanked Didier and told him to run home. 'Be a good boy!' I urged.

I waited for Jean-Claude on the pavement of the dirty, dangerous street. I said to myself that the world is revolting and man is pitiful. While I thought these and other similar thoughts, two men passed me. They turned to examine me. They were dark-skinned and wore tight trousers. Their neat bottoms reminded me of those of failed bullfighters.

Jean-Claude emerged looking pale and ravaged. He had a black eye and he was limping. It was to be a long time before I slotted this experience into others to make sense of it all.

'Your father's had a stroke,' I said, taking his arm and hurrying him along, home. I felt angry with Jean-Claude, but this was no time to show it. I imagined he had been up to something I would rather not know about. At the same time I felt I was owed an explanation.

He should have died hereafter . . . M. Guérigny's death passed almost unnoticed and unremarked, as his life had since his daughter's suicide.

'Now Maman has Montaine to herself,' Jean-Claude said without expression, adding that it would be a closer relationship than she had had with Montaine in life.

Mme Guérigny could not manage the fruit and vegetables alone. There was humping and heaving at Les Halles, and unloading and loading in the Cours Mirabeau, not to mention the display that had to be set up afresh daily. Jean-Claude

115

introduced his mother to a young unemployed Algerian who would open the *grille* at three-thirty in the morning, travel with her to Les Halles, load the van, supervise the arrangement of the produce in the Cours Mirabeau and drive the van back to the rue Victorie (when Maman was *crevée*) at one o'clock. Mme Guérigny was well satisfied with Nissim. She said of him that he had real taste with the produce and was a willing lad all round. I was surprised that Madame expressed herself so warmly when she spoke of Nissim. I wondered that her prejudices did not stretch to itinerant Arabs.

And I wondered why she was still working. She was well into her sixties, looked older, and was eligible for a pension. 'Maman is a peasant, that's why,' Jean-Claude said. Perhaps, I thought, it kept her mind occupied. Perhaps, while she hassled, she managed to forget Montaine for a few hours. But then I remembered a conversation I had overheard her having with her sister-in-law. Her daily excursions to Les Halles, she said, were precious for the opportunity they provided to visit St Eustache. In a clipped French sentence that sounded as if it had been well rehearsed, she told Agathe that she may have lost the produce of her labour but she had not lost the fruit of her labours. Of course she was a peasant. The ground of her being was the soil of France that nurtured her issue and the produce she once sowed and reaped, and now bought and sold. She had found deep, mysterious sense in the unfolding of her days. She did not need to speak her pain to any but her God. Something in me, some memory of earlier days, made me respect a woman for whom God was not only a Sunday thought. On the other hand, if for her the impossible was not merely possible, not merely probable but certain, she destroyed the route to wonder that might have enhanced her living days. She never learnt the significance of uncertainty. Despite their closeness, all this made Jean-Claude impatient with his mother. I think he saw his own inadequacies in her without making the connection. He told me once that to his mind organized religion destroyed moral and spiritual values. But I knew this was not always the case. And once when Maman was fretting over his painful joints, I heard Jean-Claude retort that it was better being a physical rather than an emotional arthritic.

It was during the period when Jean-Claude was working on the 'Chansons de Mani' that I went through the scores he wrote in la Sologne throughout his childhood and into his twenties, and others he composed in Paris before Montaine's death. All these papers had been locked away out of sight, in no particular order, in a tin trunk stored in that part of the attic which had not been incorporated into the living accommodation. When Jean-Claude took over the space for his piano, he found himself lugging the trunk into the light. He said that if I had the time and the inclination he would be grateful if I would sort through the material, put the scores in chronological order to one side and throw out 'the rubbish'.

Jean-Claude was giving me licence to determine what part of his past to conserve and what part to be rid of. Perhaps he really did want to cut loose and was restrained from so doing by Maman, who would have regarded it as disloyal. I was not yet aware of other reasons. I was Jean-Claude's gateway to the future, and I sensed he was becoming increasingly conscious of the fact, and satisfied with our relationship. Not that he said so. He did not engage in that sort of conversation. But I had learnt to understand how he felt from small things, mere comments he let slip, and from the tender power he demonstrated at night. As for myself, I was feeling a mounting confidence in my capabilities – I was of use. This proved some consolation for the ever-present insecurity Jean-Claude's secret life imposed on me.

I was astonished by the sheer quantity of stuff in the trunk. There were violin, piano and cello sonatas, quartets, concertos, and his first and only symphony. There were also dozens of songs. Many were written to lyrics by Montaine. In addition, there were papers, letters, little old boxes, all sorts of ephemera – and the type of debris found in the pockets of small boys. I felt dreadfully inadequate in the face of this material. Not only was this the evidence of a wonderful and mysterious world in which I had no place, I was being given the chance to destroy the evidence. Part of me longed to do away with all of it. The better part forbade me.

How, I wondered, was I going to find someone to judge the merit of this work objectively? Jean-Claude said no one would or could, that he was outside the influential music world: he had not attended the Conservatoire, he was a peasant without contacts. Successful composers 'knew the ropes'. He did not. 'And, anyhow, it's all in the hands of the Jews!' he told me.

I thought I would speak to Otto, ask him how best to go about having Jean-Claude's work assessed for performance. In the event, I discovered he was out of the country for a while. I was in a hurry. The promotion of Jean-Claude's music had become my *raison d'être*. I had no alternative but to consult M. Chaillot.

I agreed to go out to Passy. My need of M. Chaillot's advice put me in a weak position. I knew it. He knew it. He knew I knew it. There was no question but that Jean-Claude wanted to be a success and that it was my job to bring this about. Jean-Claude was deeply critical of all the French composers of his generation, who were receiving more attention than he was. The only living composer I heard him praise was Stravinsky; the others who met his approval were all dead. Those for whom he had the greatest contempt – a band of counterfeits – emerged from the Paris

Conservatoire and were *fils de papa. Now* I can see that I was wrong to assume that mere dedication to a craft ineluctably results in fine work, but it was that conviction which drove me to put Jean-Claude and his work on the map. He could have been composing rubbish for all I was competent to judge, yet that possibility did not enter my head.

Ça vous fait tant de plaisir et moi si peu de peine. If that was the route to Jean-Claude's success, *tant pis.*

Émile Chaillot had problems of his own, and I learnt what power a woman can achieve by satisfying bizarre sexual tastes in a man much older than herself. No wonder Mme Chaillot was so frequently out of the country. Had this been my regular field of action, I too would have made myself *hors de combat.* It was not until many years after the whole Jean-Claude episode was behind me that I realized the extent to which my physical appearance had dictated the terms of my life in Paris. I had the attributes of a boy, in that I was flat-chested, hipless and had a small bottom. Notwithstanding, I was quite obviously female. This ambiguity was much to the taste of men whose drive was probably homosexual. I am not convinced that Émile Chaillot was aware that his drive was ambivalent. I think a boyish, childlike figure – that of the *gamine* – was the one he preferred aesthetically. He could gain no satisfaction from his Rubensesque wife. Not only did her flesh disgust him, she had impregnable opinions as to what was normal sexual practice and what was not. By the time I reached my mid-twenties, being buggered about was something I simply accepted.

Émile opened the doors on Jean-Claude's success. It was a pity that such a disagreeable man had to be thanked for this. At first, I heartily disliked him. His views were anathema to me. Indeed, it was his example that led me to see beneath the brilliance and beauty of Paris, where the plight of its dispossessed is mirrored in the experience of the very people – artists and intellectuals – who are responsible for its reputation.

Émile believed himself in love with me. He regarded it as one of my most endearing qualities that I seemed to want nothing from him. He had no idea that I was prostituting myself in the cause of Jean-Claude's success. His pride could not have permitted him this simple insight. He believed that by launching Jean-Claude's music at festivals, on the radio and in small recital halls for new music, he was acquiring personal kudos. There is much profit to be gained, I calculated, from the overweening vanity of a lover.

I was surprised when, only three days after my seeing him, Émile telephoned Jean-Claude at the *pavillon* without my knowledge and proposed to him that, given his connection with la Sologne, he might like to do the music for a radio opera version of *Le Grand Meaulnes*. The libretto, which had been lying in his drawer for years, had been written by a M. Frontenac, who had known Alain-Fournier personally, and had been under the spell of his novel since it first appeared in 1913. The libretto was regarded at the radio as something of a masterpiece of translation and from time to time suitable composers had been sought. However, M. Frontenac was entitled to the final say and he had rejected a veritable Gotha of applicants before music in France became somewhat unsympathetic to a romantic text. Émile, enthusiastic about Jean-Claude's work in general (and me in particular), had sold the idea to Frontenac on the grounds of Jean-Claude's association with la Sologne.

Jean-Claude was in rapturous mood, for la Sologne was a place of elation. The opportunity to escape from Reine was irresistible. Even Mme Guérigny showed some enthusiasm for work that would take Jean-Claude back to his roots. Whilst demonstrating all too clearly her feeling that la Sologne belonged to her family, and I had no real place in it, she was able to discuss with Jean-Claude and me what we could reasonably expect from the area today, and lay down, precisely, what it was appropriate to do and not to do among the Solognats.

As a concession to his mother's tireless instructions, Jean-Claude allowed her to write to a farmer she had known, to see whether we could rent one of his cottages.

'You will come and visit us, Maman!'

'I'll see if I have the time.'

Mme Guérigny could not have borne such a thing.

LA SOLOGNE

What happens to a dream deferred?
Does it dry up like a raisin in the sun?
Or does it explode?

Langston Hughes

Much of the interior of my fate and that of Jean-Claude's was revealed to me in the opaque, vaporous interior of la Sologne.

'I need to stay as close as possible to my inner world,' Jean-Claude explained, insisting that only there was he not in exile. Inner and outer worlds coalesced, and he withdrew from me again. And so it was my experience not to become closer to him in our isolation but to approach myself more closely.

We came in summer. It was mellow, the colour of amber, never too hot. It slowed the pace of the Solognats without exhausting them. It ripened the fruit on the trees and the grapes on the vines slowly and thoroughly, and yet left the abundant streams running with clear water. Summer would have given way to autumn imperceptibly, had it not been that autumn was the hunting season, and hunting the very purpose of the region. Visitors descended from far and wide on the *auberges* and the châteaux. Shots peppered the air. Guns stood stacked outside the café, the *épicerie* and the *boulangerie*. There was a smell of game and metal in the air, and bustle where so recently there had been calm. The lords of the *manoirs* and their servants converged as they had in medieval times.

Winter was exceptionally hard: icy cold and damp, all life arrested. The terrain being flat, the wind tore across scrub and heathland unimpeded, and the snow it drove ahead of itself banked against our cottage, so that to get out to the pump we had to dig ourselves a path. Reaching the village across the sea of dazzling snow was impossible by motor cycle, and often difficult on foot. I learnt to look ahead so as not to run out of stores.

Spring unfolded sweetly pale. The field in front of the cottage was of indefinable colour, the grasses stained with the delicate tones of buttercups, primroses and cowslips. I rose with the sun to gather mushrooms. Throughout the day I left the cottage door open. Ducks and chickens from the farm brought their young into the kitchen.

I learnt how to occupy myself. This was the first time in my life that I had lived in deep country, without easy access to shops, transport and people I knew. We had no running water, no electricity, no gas. As an urban creature I had dubbed these conditions 'inconvenient' and 'primitive'. But little by little, as I became absorbed into rural life, I came to enjoy my 'inconveniences'. Because everything took a long time to complete, I started to savour occupations which in the past I had regarded as chores to be endured.

My favourite expedition was the one I always made alone, to the farm. I bought our dairy produce and our vegetables from Mme Deloche. I varied the days and the times of my visits so as to catch this resourceful woman at her different occupations, for example making the wild boar and hind sausages, for which she was renowned in the neighbourhood, and the tarts filled with medlars that grew against the wall of her stable. Mme Deloche became my mentor during this period, and for years after I left France, I used to send her Oxford Marmalade, Bath Olivers and Christmas puddings in exchange for the things she had taught me to make. For it was with Mme Deloche that I discussed the little book I had started putting together in Paris: *Cooking with Difficulty*. It was one thing to have mastered cooking on two electric rings when the *boulangerie, charcuterie* and *épicerie* were five minutes distant, quite another to keep a range alight, bake bread and manage slow-cooking food. Mme Deloche taught me the basics I needed to learn.

As soon as we settled in la Sologne, I started to study *Le Grand Meaulnes*. I remembered the sort of questions Father used to ask me when I was reading a book he knew by heart, and greatly loved. And wanted me to love. *Le Grand Meaulnes* was short, and I had it by heart quite quickly. I needed to, for Jean-Claude remembered it word for word. I noticed Alain-Fournier's particular obsession with the weather. He made it cling to the garments of his characters to provide them with something of their personalities. I noticed, too, something that surprised me: an abundance of images of the sea. For this is a thoroughly land-locked story in land-locked country. Must adventure always be connected with getting far away, over the sea, to foreign places? And how would Jean-Claude interpret this? And what music is there for waterlogged fields? Enclosed? For albescent mist and rivers running with fish?

'Everything points to escape by sea,' he told me wistfully, in response to my questions.

Our cottage stood in a field at the opposite end of the village from the smallholding the Guérigny family used to work. I believe the disposition of the rooms and the view we had was much like the one Jean-Claude had had throughout his childhood. Whereas in Reine Jean-Claude reminded me of a caged animal, in Préfleur he reminded me of something growing in its natural habitat. I watched him, unobserved, at work. I watched his physiognomy change, making him appear now old and furrowed, with veins bulging at the temples, now youthful as a boy. It was as if his seasons came and went in the phrases he wrote. He sat at the table at the upstairs window, as Montaine used to sit in her room in the smallholding, overlooking a view much like the one she loved over heathland towards the forest. He wrote with her pen and kept the little envelope filled with notes she used to write him by his side. Sometimes, when I was downstairs cooking or reading, I imagined I heard a piano playing, so keenly did I feel Montaine's presence.

It was late summer when Otto joined us. He came by train to Romorantin and Jean-Claude rode to the station to meet him. Arriving back at the cottage, Otto was in a thoroughly excited state. He said pillion riding was one of the most exhilarating experiences he knew of. I hoped the simplicity of our living accommodation was not going to be a horrible disappointment to him.

The cottage had one sizeable room above two others, one of which had been reclaimed from its original function as byre for the cow and converted into a scullery, with a copper and sink which drained straight into the field. The cottage had not been inhabited for a while. It smelt of stored apples and herbs. The range stood in the kitchen/living-room. It had a personality of its own: that of an aged and obstinate peasant. It was intended to provide not only a means of cooking but of heating the water we drew from the well. The range performed these duties, but with a certain reluctance, and I wondered how Otto would put up with a mere cup of water to shave in. And although I infinitely preferred a walk across the corner of the field to the privy by the duck pond, to the four flights of stairs I had to descend at Reine, with a communal Turkish crouch at the end of it, I wondered how Otto would adjust to outside facilities.

He was to sleep on the sofa. Fortunately the ancient piece of furniture that answered to 'sofa' lacked an arm. He would be able to stretch his legs out over the end. I tested the springs as best I could, but I weighed under seven stone and Otto was tall and well built. I wondered how comfortable he would be and what he would make of the covers I had borrowed from the farmer's wife. They were clearly a family treasure. They had been salted away in mothballs and smelt of naphthalene. I found them extraordinarily beautiful. They were made from six-inch squares of crochet work, sewn together, each square a different colour and texture, made, I supposed, from odd ends of wool conserved by generations of thrifty peasants.

I went into the field and gathered autumn leaves and flowers and put them in jam jars around the cottage. I swept and scrubbed, and cleaned the windows. I thought the cottage looked lovely – settled, solid, timeless. I changed into a dress. Jean-Claude had warned me that Otto would want to spend some time at the gastronomic festival being held in Romorantin. I should not expect them back before late in the afternoon. I pushed open the window. In the distance I heard the crackle of gun-shot.

Jean-Claude's working table stood under the window upstairs where we slept and stored our few clothes. I never touched this table. I did not so much as flick a duster around the papers. It was pure chance that made me notice the writing on the top file, as I pushed open the window. It read: 'Le Grand Meaulnes. An opera for radio. Text and music by Jean-Claude Guérigny from the novel by Alain-Fournier.' I was puzzled. The commission that had brought us to Préfleur was for music to a libretto by M. Xavier Frontenac. I picked up the file and stood with it in my hands for a few minutes before deciding whether to examine its contents. And then I sat down on the bed and opened it.

Page one was headed NOTES ONLY. There followed fourteen pages divided under headings.

LOCATIONS
(1) Sainte-Agathe – farms, *Café Daniel, petits coins, vieille planche*, square, church . . .
(2) Les Sablonnières.
(3) Countryside (N.B. weather).
CHARACTERS
(1) François Seurel, narrator, mostly *sprechgesang* to set scenes, describe locations and weather. Tenor.
(2) M. Seurel. Bass.
(3) Mme Millie Seurel. Sop.
(4) Meaulnes. Light baritone.
(5) Yvonne de Galais. Sop.
(6) Frantz de Galais.?
(7) Valentine. Mezzo-Sop.
(8) Children, vagabonds, peasants, etc.

MUSIC

La Sologne: consider 'Transfigured Night'. *Bruitage musical* for village life: birdsong, cocks crowing, pigs grunting, cows lowing, horses being shod, cows being milked, hens' necks being wrung, wood being cut, etc. Café clutter: tinkle of glass, ring of china, men's voices at dominoes and darts. Wagons and carriages over soft and hard ground. Sabots on the gravel. Shots being fired by hunters. Shop life: tinkle of money, rustle of notes, voices. School life: Millie's kitchen sounds, plus sewing-machine. Children's voices, objects being hurled about schoolroom, books banged shut, games of chase, etc.

WATER: land-locked region filled with water. Running in streams, stagnant in ponds, drawn from wells. Rain. Storm. Tears. Sobs.

LIGHT: albescent.

MOODS: adventurous, sick, deathly, loving.

N.B. Find memorable tune for Frantz's call. Incorp. into leitmotif. Hammer on anvil, sparks flying. Piano music to link Millie/Yvonne/Mme Meaulnes = domestic happiness.

SYNOPSIS: a quest to return to lost paradise of childhood. The land without a name – silent, deep, useless.

LOCATION: la Sologne (Alain-Fournier country).

PLOT: young idealist, adventurer, absconds from school in Sainte-Agathe, finds himself in mysterious domain with crumbling château where a wedding party (organized by children) is under way. Whole village present – rich, poor; some in fancy dress. Atmosphere festive, real/unreal, dreamlike. Boating party. Feast. Party disbands because groom and fiancée (Frantz and Valentine) do not turn up. Meanwhile, Meaulnes has seen and fallen in love with a beautiful woman, who grants him permission to return one day. She will be waiting . . . Meaulnes returns to school. Refuses to say where he has been and what has happened: *must protect perfection of his dreamlike adventure. This sets him apart from the ordinary and gives him a reason for living.*

STORY: how Meaulnes gets back to the lost domain. Why he leaves. Affair with Valentine. Betrayal of Frantz. Guilt. Ambivalent conclusion. Objective: revelation of truth.

Between pages of dialogue were interspersed ideas for the music with which Jean-Claude would link episodes and characterize individuals. I was conscious of rich chaos, the sort of jumble that lures one into a junk-shop knowing that under the piles of objects and above one's head there are riches to be mined. At the back of the notes, tucked into a folder, I found Xavier Frontenac's libretto. Neat and logical as a four-times table, M. Frontenac had stuck doggedly to the sequence of events in Alain-Fournier's story. Jean-Claude, on the other hand, understood that the logic of the dream-world was not that of the actual world. He would ignore chronology for the sake

135

of truth. I felt apprehensive, however. I knew that Frontenac had certain rights to the material and Jean-Claude had none. Émile Chaillot had not commissioned a libretto from Jean-Claude.

I stacked the papers carefully and replaced them where I had found them. I wandered out into the field. The pale sun was low in the sky, a few birds celebrated, otherwise the quiet was tangible. I understood how and why Jean-Claude had so enthusiastically taken on this work. Not only did it free him from Reine, it returned him to Préfleur. His childhood idyll was his to relive. He was rescued from his exile in adulthood. And all this was reflected in a book of genius he was going to translate and embellish for his own ends. He had made the point: he was going to strengthen the musical possibilities of his opera by creating a sound picture of paradise from which would bleed the eventualities of the real and actual world. His own life would be both source and reflection of his work. In another note – in the margin of his description of the characters – he had scribbled: 'all three male ch. aspects of a single man=author'. I noticed nothing to suggest this insight in Frontenac's version of the story. And Frontenac was not a Solognat. Jean-Claude had made several attempts before to encapsulate the land of la Sologne in music. He was not going to forgo the opportunity of adding to his music the force of his words.

★   ★   ★

Otto struck me as looking so out of place as to seem absurd, standing at the cottage door trying to approve our living accommodation, but clearly regarding it as unpromising. 'Charming! Charming, my dear!' he muttered through closed teeth, throwing his Louis Vuitton overnight case on to the sofa. '*Opal, ma petite, embrasse-moi!*'

It was just warm enough for us to sit at the table outside and drink cool wine in the fading sun. I had not realized how well Otto knew the area. He mentioned a lake not far away, at the centre of which a farmer had placed a scarecrow. Otto had provided an old dinner-jacket for it. He always wanted to 'inform'. He told me of the way the rivers were kept permanently netted for fish, of the illnesses associated with la Sologne, and of its politics. He had visited the landmarks of Jean-Claude's childhood some years before, and every year (sadly, not this year) he shot on the Comte de Something-or-Other's land, where the ploughing was still done with horses. Otto and Jean-Claude exchanged cherished memories. Jean-Claude's went back to the time when the region was awash with oceans of rye, Otto's to the time when the Demoiselles Tatin were still alive.

We walked for an hour without passing a single habitation. We crossed over heathland and passed ponds crowded with rushes and bordered by willows. We followed a winding, sandy lane strewn with yellowing pine needles and, just before entering the forest, sighted a *manoir* with tall towers reminiscent of candle-snuffers. The pink brick and grey slate was catching the dying rays of the sun. And then we opened a gate into the woods.

Our first sight of the restaurant was one of lanterns twinkling through the dusk. The building reminded me of a conservatory, the walls being made from small panes of glass. Inside and outside converged; it was possible to forget that the lanterns were not the stars. I remember what we ate: *cèpes* in cream and herbs, partridges in vine leaves, the *Tartouillat* – a delicious strudel-like pastry filled with pumpkin and apples. As was usual with Otto, the conversation revolved around what we were consuming. However, on this occasion – because of Jean-Claude's roots in this countryside – it extended to a discussion of all the food of la Sologne.

'. . . but there's no *grande cuisine* here! Rich and poor eat the same dishes . . .'

'I'd hardly say that! Maman used to have to fill us up with *la miausée*.' And Jean-Claude made a face and described a gruel made from rye bread. 'But, of course, like everyone, Papa got game off the land and fish from the ponds, and there were always the different sorts of mushrooms, and the trees were absolutely laden with chestnuts, medlars and pears . . .' His tone changed abruptly when Otto intoned 'paradise'. 'Hardly that! My family knew that however long and however hard they worked to scrape a living, they would always be poor. Just because the land was generous and never left them seriously hungry, it didn't mean they were ever relieved of their relentless toil. And we grew up puny, with bad chests. Papa had stomach ulcers . . .'

Otto knew when to change the subject. 'I remember when Proust's '*Bon Chrétien*' flourished. Now those pears made a truly memorable tart. Alas, they are a fruit of yesteryear.' By now I knew the identity of this Mr Proust, who cropped up in conversations as if he were a much-revered bachelor uncle. 'And of course, when Madame was still with us I used to enjoy her *Tarte Tatin* at the eponymous hotel . . .'

Otto was speaking – spluttering would be more apt a description – with his mouth full. He lacked the skill to talk without revealing the hashed contents of his meal. I noticed this with distaste, and rejoiced that it was not the asparagus season. I had once had to witness Otto tackling a bundle in Paris and it left a lasting impression: of an elephant stripping bark.

Despite these reflections we were relaxed, even content. We had drunk a lot more than was usual for Jean-Claude and me, and we rolled slowly back to the cottage, stopping only, on Jean-Claude's insistence, to listen to the music of the night insects. 'Listen . . . ssh . . .' And he flashed his torch and gathered fluttering moths in the beam. Then, lowering the light, he guided us along the banks of a stream to a pond. The dank smell of the water was not unpleasant, and for years the scent of la Sologne that enveloped me that night would pierce my memory: a combination of stagnant water, slime, wild mushrooms, wispy dry grasses, sand and well-hung game. The still dark that night had the effect of making everything heavy with meaning.

Jean-Claude sat in his usual position for the job, his knees wide apart, grinding the coffee-beans. Otto and I started on the marc Otto had brought as a present.

'*Ce petit con*, Frontenac! I ask myself whether Chaillot ever glanced at his libretto, let alone read it. It's unsingable, for one thing. And for another, he's tried to get the whole book in, just as it's written. Quite the wrong approach – all bulk, no weight. I scrapped the idea of doing the music for it after ten pages. I'm doing something of my own.' Jean-Claude spoke in bursts between the laborious and exhausting grinding on his ancient machine, which he complained strained his arm.

'Will Chaillot accept that?'

'If he knows what's good for him he will.'

'I'm not at all sure he likes being told.' And Otto laughed.

'My music is so much better than anyone else's. They are making big names for themselves with pap. *Ce petit con*, Dubois, *et ce petit con*, Devaux – they give the public what it expects . . . That's not my way.' (And indeed it was not. Before I knew Jean-Claude, he had performed a piece for piano in which he repeated for seven minutes a single twelve-note phrase at thirty-second intervals. He explained he had wanted his audience to sit on the edge of their seats, hoping and believing that the composer was going to amplify his idea – and then to confound them. 'They didn't know how to listen without expectation,' he told me. In the event, they rose from their seats, booed and shuffled out to the box-office, where they demanded their money back without success. Émile Chaillot, however, did remain seated, a restraining hand on his wife's arm. And he applauded at the end of the recital. A few other members of the music world – too embarrassed or well mannered to have left – applauded with him. The critics had a field-day. Some denounced Jean-Claude for insulting his public, others praised him for respecting them. 'I'm controversial, you understand.')

Not wishing to find myself involved in contention, I excused myself and went upstairs to bed before the coffee ritual was completed. But I could not sleep. Otto's voice shot through the gaps in the floorboards in a series of volleys, Jean-Claude's less assured tones seeped through. I pulled the sheet over my head and tried not to piece their words into sentences I would not want to hear. And when their voices dropped and silenced, I put my fingers in my ears, for I did not want to hear that, either.

But still I could not sleep. I sat at the open window and looked out on to the purple dark. I was conscious – I think, for the first time – that beauty would never distract me from my anxieties. I wanted Jean-Claude. I wanted him with me there and then. I did not want him to be alone with Otto. The blood pooled between my thighs.

'. . . he's very depressed . . . see him when I can . . . he's not working . . . not doing anything, much . . . still lies about in that appalling house drinking . . . I'm the only non-resident of the rue de Sèvres he admits . . .'

'. . . I know . . . he'll never get over it . . . never . . .'

I moved from the window and stood over a gaping crack in the floorboards and listened hard. Jean-Claude was telling Otto that Ahmed could not imagine loving another woman. That on the one hand he felt that to do so would be a betrayal, and on the other, an impossibility: how was he to find another woman as pure, as mysteriously beautiful?

'He's livid about Opal.' Otto laughed.

'I know, I know all about that,' Jean-Claude replied without emotion. 'The last time I saw him he'd been drinking pretty heavily and he pushed me about a bit. I don't think he meant me harm, but somehow I hit the corner of the wardrobe and got myself a black eye and one or two other bruises . . .'

'He doesn't seem to be writing.'

'How could he, the state he's in?'

'That book of his, though, it's still doing quite well. I noticed it in the window of La Hune only last week.'

'He's still getting a little money from it. He told me in one of his more lucid states that he can't write because he's got too much to say . . .'

'That is sometimes worse than having too little,' Otto agreed.

'He talks of the void. He says the present is so empty, it's as if she never existed. Death is not the end of a life for him but its denial. I don't understand him. She's always with me. Sometimes I forget her face but remember something more unchanging. I take her with me, everywhere. We used to be alone together in the midst of the world . . .'

'I think he feels humiliated as much as grief-stricken. For an Arab to be refused by his amour . . .'

With the misery of the dead Montaine's love affair to relieve my suspicions, I fell asleep. Now that I knew the source of Jean-Claude's black eye and bruises, I felt lighter, and the chasm of distrust that had been opened up between Jean-Claude and myself in the rue de Sèvres, closed with the key Otto had unwittingly provided.

We had returned to the land without a name – the lost paradise of childhood. It was not merely a state of mind, it was a real location in the heart of France. This was where Jean-Claude belonged: on the desolate sandy heaths that break against distant shores of pines; by pools of still water fringed with reeds and willows; on stony paths ground by wagon wheels. His whole and deepest self was so drenched in the brooding melancholy of la Sologne as to make his years in Paris seem unreal. And the most dazzling evidence of his vitality was the death of his sister. Her death, and the pain it wrought in him, now generated the work which was his memorial to their youthful love. He may have been dependent on me for the time being for his physical well-being, but at the deepest level he was dependent on Montaine. Could some only love until death parted them?

'I have been in exile far too long,' Jean-Claude told me. And so saying, he led me over the fields to his childhood home.

The Guérignys' smallholding on the edge of the village of Préfleur had fallen into dilapidation; the roof of the red, herring-bone-brick house and stabling had caved in, leaving the ribs exposed and the heart shattered. The garden, which had provided not only subsistence but a little cash crop, was over-grown with brambles and cow-parsley and other vegetation of interest only to wildlife. In one field the soil was arid; nothing seemed able to grow there but a sort of grass that even sheep disdained, and thistles a hobbled donkey was sampling. The pond water was strangled with poisonous weed. Beneath the weed the water lay inert. No carp, no pike survived. I learnt then from Jean-Claude that the property had never belonged to the family. It had been rented for generations from a local landowner.

'Peasant poverty was the most powerful reality

my family knew. We never imagined things could get better. Not a week of my childhood passed without some mention of the disaster of 1880, when a particularly cruel winter laid waste thirty years' vegetation. That catastrophe was ever imminent, ready to strike again. But,' and he paused to look about him and sigh, 'this is my land.' It was a fate he not only accepted but embraced.

And so I could not be certain whether the sight of his old home depressed him more than it inspired him. I wondered whether the fact that the buildings had collapsed, were no longer the ordered haven of childhood, helped him to understand that whatever he might do to reinstate the fabric of the place, he would not succeed in re-creating the past. I remember, too, wondering what part the imminence of its destruction had in making paradise so sweet.

Jean-Claude insisted to me more than once that to transpose *Le Grand Meaulnes* it was essential to have had a childhood like his own. And it was obvious Frontenac had not.

'He seems to have no feeling for the narrow plank one walks between fulfilment and stalemate . . . for mystery, for hope and wonder. He can't make the point that trying to hang on to those feelings leads to unbearable frustration. That's the experience I must render! I must revive in the listening public their own sense of moving about in worlds unrealized . . . The only country worth trying to get to is Utopia, Opal, but one has to understand . . .

It's not what I believe in or what I can see and touch that's the most important, it's the unseen reality behind physical appearances . . . That's it – what eludes me, what eludes Meaulnes. What we both yearn for. The real world bordered by our sleep.'

And then I started to understand at some deep level that it is not only the dream-world one desires but the world one imagines. And I did not find this revelation consoling.

Jean-Claude spoke of his plans to reinstate the Guérigny house and stables with the money he would receive for his opera. The landowner was letting the buildings return to dust, but no doubt he would be grateful to have them restored at no cost to himself. Jean-Claude's excitement made me anxious. I could see how all his plans might well come to nothing. I had to speak to Émile.

A few days later I rang Émile. He was delighted to hear from me. 'How are you surviving the desert?' he inquired.

'I love it.'

'And how is the great man's work proceeding?'

'Well. Really well.'

'*Ma petite Opal*, could you not slip away, just for the day?'

As luck would have it, Jean-Claude found he needed some old scores he had put to one side as they were too heavy to bring along with everything else we had had to load on the motor cycle.

146

His work was going well. He did not want to interrupt it. If he rode me over to Romorantin to catch the early train to Paris, would I mind going out to Reine for him? He would meet me off the last train . . .

Émile permitted himself the luxury of imagining I had come to Paris just to see him. He took me to lunch at a discreetly ill-lit restaurant and then to an hotel on the Ile St Louis, where we passed two hours of the afternoon gratifying his fantasies. I waited until I had showered, dressed and repaired my make-up before raising my anxiety.

'I think I should warn you: Jean-Claude's not writing music to Frontenac's libretto. He's doing the whole thing himself – words and music.'

'That's not what I commissioned.'

'I know. But I do think that what he's doing is something truly wonderful – and quite different. He's using a lot of natural sounds – kitchen percussion, crowd voices . . . all sorts of new devices . . . I'm sure it'll create a stir.'

'That's not the point. The rights are Frontenac's. The estate won't allow it. He can use his "devices", as you call them, in something else, but you must stop him, *ma petite Opal.* He's wasting his time and mine.' Émile Chaillot displayed the deep impatience of a bureaucrat towards an artist who is not doing as he is bid. Artists were an occupational hazard that Émile would do without if only he could. 'I shan't pay him!' Indeed, he would

147

demand the advance back. 'Look, get him to ring me. Use your exquisite charm and deviousness, little one . . .'

And then I agreed to do something for Émile that I did not wish to do, which made me ashamed.

'What a lovely little thing you are!'

'Émile dear, you know the success of Jean-Claude's opera will be much to your credit,' I purred. 'He's your protégé.'

It was the day of the pilgrimage. Jean-Claude must have been planning it since we arrived, but he did not mention it until the day before. He was going to take me to the derelict château he and Montaine had discovered in a clearing in one of the forests. We were to go on foot so as not to disturb the tranquillity.

We set out before 7 a.m., but Jean-Claude did not tell me how far away the château stood, or how long it would take to reach the boundary of the domain. He said it was quite a way – the other side of Préfleur, towards the hills, and that we would catch sight of the white gateposts from a distance. 'The château itself is secreted behind beech trees.' And then he described to me the first time he and Montaine had happened upon it.

'It was an unforgettable experience, accompanied by a feeling of absolute contentment, utter serenity. I've never had quite that feeling since. A bird flew above us, as if guiding us. It repeated the same three-note phrase over and over, and

Montaine caught the little tune and sang it back.' Jean-Claude whistled the phrase and then hummed it. It was becoming a leitmotif in his opera, he said. 'It must have been spring. I can see in my mind's eye the avenue of chestnuts alight with red and white candles. We glimpsed the château from very far. We were at the summit of the hangers, and the long, low building of white stone was crouched in the valley. It had two wings, one of which made me think of a church. When we got up to the place, we found it was un-inhabited. Some of the glass in the windows was broken, a huge door stood ajar. I took Montaine by the hand and led her through the empty rooms . . . there were very many. We were not used to large houses . . . In one of the rooms we found trunks of clothes. We dressed up in them. There were mirrors everywhere in which we preened ourselves as we became prince and princesse, duc and duchesse. We played at giving parties and balls and having gargantuan feasts. We imagined the little rooms were for story-telling, and the vast rooms for the horses and hounds. We played circuses. We called out from where we hid in different rooms and listened to our voices echo, we strummed on the few keys left on a rotting piano, and plucked at a broken lute . . . Birds had built their nests and raised their young in the once ordered kitchens. Water had flowed into the now cracked bath-tubs. Linen and lace had rotted into cobwebs on the beds, where now there were only twisted brass bones. By the time we had exhausted the building, it was late. The rabbits were out feeding in the fields. We looked back at the crumbling house. The wing that had appeared like a church from afar was clutched in the attenuated arms of a vine, held up by the vine like a drunken dancer in the arms of a lover.

'Through frothy spring and sun-drenched summer we returned to play in secret. We only stopped when the weather made it impossible: the snow confused us and we couldn't find our way. But just once – it was to be the last time – we did get back. We followed in the tracks of hares. We didn't go into the house. That was not what we wanted. We just needed to make sure the place existed and was not a dream. We went to the back, to the great stone pond, to see what had happened to the fish. We hung over the rim and were stared back at by our reflections, horribly deformed in the cracks of the thin ice. We couldn't have understood the message, but we sensed undisclosed meaning and were afraid. The air was so cold we could hardly breathe it. The feeling left our fingers and toes. We clung together for warmth and vowed to love one another more than anyone else for all time. How dangerous that turned out to be! But we were children . . . very young . . . I can't remember how young. And we were pure.'

Jean-Claude had taken me along a lane that struck out towards a château it fell short of reaching. Not on that day or on any other day did he attempt such a sortie with me.

I walked some way behind Jean-Claude on the narrow path that skirted the woods and lost sight of him when my attention was diverted to a shadowy path in the trees. There I noticed a bent peasant in black, creeping ghostlike under a load of kindling. Théovard! I felt uneasy. When I caught up with Jean-Claude, he told me to return to the cottage alone.

The silence that enclosed me made me feel the world had come to an end, that the trees had not yet been informed but soon would be, and would fall on to the stone and thorn, the heather and the fern, skeletons to be picked over, not by vultures but by time. And that would be that: thousands of years of generation succeeding generation, unable to learn from the experience of the past and dying too soon to benefit from the present.

Above all other expeditions I had wanted to complete this one – to follow in the footsteps of Jean-Claude and his beloved sister, and regain their paradise. But I was an intruder, a trespasser on a past that was as much place as time. To have urged Jean-Claude would have seemed indecent. To have insisted would have been to demand more details about Montaine, and more explanations about their love, than I was entitled to. Indeed, I wondered whether it was possible for someone who had not shared in their experience to pass physically through the white gateposts into the avenue, and attain the domain.

Such a consideration did not arise in connection

with Sainte-Agathe, however, and when Jean-Claude felt he needed to refresh his memory of details, we rode cross-country to the village. We left the motor cycle propped against the railings of the school, the long red building festooned with Virginia creeper where Alain-Fournier, as well as his characters, had been a pupil. We checked on the five french windows that opened on to the playground, noted the survival of the wash-house and, on walking to the side of the school and round the back, found the original planks that constituted the *vieille planche* intact. I wandered alone across the muttering stream and satisfied myself that the spongy land was still lined with alders. But the farm, the Belle-Etoile, was not where I expected to find it. I felt disorientated; I discovered the farm was actually on the other side of the school, across the lane. In vain I sought the ducks penned in safety from the foxes . . .

The village was deserted. No sigh of bellows, no glare of a charcoal blaze: the double doors of the farrier stood shut. Other doors and windows were flung wide open, but no sound emerged from them. The sun was hot and bright. We sauntered to the crossroads – the 'four roads' – at the other end of the village and entered the Café Daniel, a mean place without character, its ceiling smoked ochre with nicotine. We ordered lemon syrups with ice-cold water, and drank standing at the bar. A few labourers drifted in, muttered good-day and threw back Poire William, as if it were purely medicinal. I found the café depressing, and walked to the open door and watched a goose waddle down the lane, her goslings in obedient Indian file. Jean-Claude caught up with me. We walked away from the house of the *notaire*, with its brass-studded door, and passed a haystacked stable where a horse, steam rising from its coat, stamped its feet at us. And then we searched out the *petits coins*, a place described as 'more asleep than the rest of the village'. And so it was, even on that somnolent day. The men who occupied the little boxlike houses were day workers, hired for the fields. Their womenfolk shut themselves behind closed doors and windows to weave their cloth and sew their clothes. They had no time to chatter in the lane. No time to make concessions to the weather. And I remembered it was here the dumb woman lived. I shuddered. The rue de Sèvres came to mind. We walked on towards the church with the bulbous steeple. The belfry was ringing out cheerfully over the square. We sat down on the little grass patch where the strolling players set up their tent. We did not talk much. Jean-Claude made some notes and sang some snatches and beat out percussion ideas on the ground with an alder switch. A cloud of pigeons rose over the poplars, and scattered. And then I was aware of deep silence. The bells had stopped ringing.

On our return journey, we rode through a village where the houses, like ships, were moored along a canal and could be approached only over little bridges. As we rode on and emerged into open country a mist was hanging some feet above the ground, as if suspended by a conjuror.

'Shall I rinse you?' I was crouched in the tin bath soaping myself in front of the range. Jean-Claude half filled a pitcher with pump-water and added hot water from the huge kettle on the hob. Carefully, delicately he rinsed the suds from my body, and taking a bath sheet wrapped me in it.

In the silent happiness that was life in la Sologne, Jean-Claude explained to me why he was not working on Frontenac's libretto and how he would not do so for any amount of money. He did not know I had read his notes and I did not confess I had, but he elaborated on what I had read, and I was convinced he had right on his side – if not prudence.

I suggested it would be a good idea to talk to Émile Chaillot before he did any more work. 'What if he demands the advance back?' I asked, somewhat disingenuously. I hated to raise the subject. I did not want Jean-Claude to think I thought of his work only in terms of the money it might earn.

In the event, he just shrugged. 'Look! This is *my* subject because it's *my* land. I know every blade of grass, fern, broom, every tree, pond and lane for miles around. Frontenac only knows what he's read of the place. And because he daren't leave out anything, he never gets anything crucial in.

He doesn't understand what *Le Grand Meaulnes* is all about. To give you an example, he simply leaves out Meaulnes's obligations to Frantz. If he can't understand a man's obligation to a friend, how can he understand a man's love for a woman? I just won't work on anything so superficial.'

It was then that it occurred to me that there was some connection between Jean-Claude's relationship with Ahmed and Meaulnes's with Frantz. I did not understand perfectly what the connection was but I felt guilt was involved – and a sense of obligation.

There was no question of his telephoning Émile Chaillot: he was not going to take orders from a mere administrator. In many ways, I knew his uncompromising attitude was the right one, but I also knew that if Frontenac owned the rights to the novel as librettist, Jean-Claude's version would be stillborn. For music to lie in a drawer is death without birth . . . Because Jean-Claude must have felt all this, too, there was no point in my saying anything. His singlemindedness was something only he could deal with. I got on with some work of my own and he went back to his.

He worked all day on his opera, stopping only to eat and stroll out, alone, into the field. He was preoccupied and spoke less and less. I was grateful for the radio he had borrowed from the farmer, although I had to play it almost inaudibly, so as not to disturb him. I got on with *Cooking with Difficulty. I* was grateful to have this work to do.

I was absorbed by it. But not once did Jean-Claude ask me about it. If I mentioned it to him I could see he was bored to the point of distress. '*Bon!*' was all he said. '*Bon!*' as he pushed back his chair after a meal and made for the stairs and his own preoccupations.

It was one thing for Jean-Claude to have had the experiences that made him uniquely suited to interpret Alain-Fournier's novel; it was quite another for those experiences to have laid the foundations for a creative, *personal* life. Although he might well spend his days in one place, obsessively devoted to music-making, he would always be morally underemployed. It is easier, in some ways, to labour with the past than the present. It is easier to take moral instruction from a character in a book than think it out oneself.

It had been Mme Guérigny's and Montaine's intimacy with the creatures of the forest that had given them the idea of hiding their deserter in the cave. To regain his sanctuary, we had to push deep into the forest. *En route,* we passed a woodman baking potatoes and chestnuts on the ashes of a fire, as Jean-Claude had done, and a huge swarm of angry, iridescent flies hovering over a dead fox, as he had been accustomed to finding close at hand. It was some time before Jean-Claude found the place he was looking for. Brambles and nettles concealed the opening. It was only because he had noticed a tree with a particular marking carved into the trunk, which he had himself incised, that he found the cave at all. He took out his knife and cut a swathe to the hollow. I waited while he jumped down into the clearing and disappeared. I felt a peculiar apprehension, and sensed the woodland spirits of which Mme Guérigny lived in awe. When Jean-Claude emerged from the hide-out, he held out his arm and dragged me into the dark cave. I could see by the light of his torch that the cave was deep and spacious; I could not make out from the beam of light its total dimensions, but clearly a man would have had no problem stretching out to sleep there. And during daylight hours Jean-Claude told me he used to sit con-cealed in the hollow in front of the cave. It was there he read and wrote. He talked rather obses-sively about those times, and while he talked I was overwhelmed by feelings of desolation: this no man's land made me uneasy. I wanted to flee.

I was astonished, therefore, when Jean-Claude sighed and said: 'Those were the days!'

I looked up at him. I noticed how he had slipped his feet under the exposed roots of trees – them-selves held in the grasp of the hollow. Surely, I thought, he cannot be reflecting with pleasure on days of danger and incarceration? But he was: with a sort of ecstasy.

'I can feel her presence, even now. She used to ride over on a white mare she borrowed and tether it somewhere over there by that tree.' The thought of Montaine was so arresting that for a moment he could not speak. He pointed. 'The undergrowth was quite short in those days.' Once again, he stopped speaking, as if winded. 'I saw the face of Eve in Eden. She was so lovely. You can't imagine how lovely she was. She always wore white . . . In my memory it is always white . . .'

We walked back wordlessly, the silence sounding deeper as we snapped twigs underfoot. The air was filled with the scent of beech nuts and rotted leaves. A shy doe stood stock-still, observing us from no more than a few feet away. The leaves in the canopy trembled in the breeze, as if conversing soundlessly. Emerging into the field, I heard a dog howl in the distance.

Living as he was on the borders of his lost paradise, in the limitless landscape of childhood from which he had been banished into adulthood, an uncomfortable country, I sensed that Jean-Claude was continually grappling with the feeling that his present was a poor reflection of his past. He had no language for his sense of exile but his music, which would not be transmitted. I felt rather desperate for him. I could not tell to which world he belonged, the past or the present. He seemed to me to be at the mercy of waves that tossed him back and forth between then and now: the real-and-actual and the desired. The adventure on which he had embarked, which was to give a sort of permanence to the past, was the one thing that kept him anchored to a chair and table all day, and often into the night. The Guérigny house was crumbling into the ground, the garden was overgrown; the cave had been bequeathed to the beasts of the forest. I do not know whether he went back to the château on his own. I suspect he did not because he could not. Like all else, the crumbling fabric must have mouldered into the ground of time, wiped from the face of the earth, turned from the quick to dust. Montaine was dead. Mme Guérigny was committed to mourning. Only music persisted – and that for a winding-sheet.

I did not exist for Jean-Claude as a separate human being with needs of my own. I knew this and I knew it was a weakness in him and I should not put up with it. Yet despite it I experienced a sort of expectation. A powerful electric current would pass through me and launch a surge of excitement: something wonderful awaited me. I felt it when I caught sight of Jean-Claude unobserved, or as I reflected on him when he was out of sight. Somehow this charge generated itself involuntarily; it was not a reaction to anything with which Jean-Claude provided me. For although our nights' experiences were equally shared and celebrated, our days were incongruent. By day, I merely served Jean-Claude. I provided the calm, the cleanliness, the order and nourishment that made it possible for him to work. And he accepted these conditions believing, no doubt (if he thought of it at all), that I fulfilled myself by providing the conditions he as an artist needed. But I started to question my submission. It was not only Jean-Claude's selfishness that struck me, but my collusion in it. I was living as if dependent upon his need of me. Severed as I was from Father and from Helmut, living in a foreign country, was it the fear of further severance that kept me in this unequal concurrence?

It was with these thoughts that I returned alone to the cottage. I seemed to be detached from myself, watching myself as I sat spooning sugar into my cup, seeing the brown liquid absorb the solid grains, thinking about the incidents of my life that clogged the flow of time. I seemed to be standing still. My life was being timed but I was not contributing. And then, for an instant, time reversed. I heard children's voices and imagined the château where a fancy-dress party was in full swing. The windows of the cottage streamed with sunblood.

Jean-Claude returned after dark. A little wind had been born from the breeze and was sighing in the walnut tree and rattling the scullery door. Jean-Claude was restless. He paced up and down between the scullery and the living-room as if on the deck of a ship. I encouraged him to bed. We lay coiled like snakes, listening to the wind gathering force to rage into a storm.

I knew a letter had come for him. I saw the hired hand from M. Deloche's farm coming across the field with it in his hand. I heard Jean-Claude thud down the stairs and greet the man at the door.

No more than an hour passed before Jean-Claude came to me in the scullery and said he would be away for a few days.

'It's Montaine's friend, Ahmed. He needs me. He's not well. I promised, you see, I promised I'd go to him if he asked. I owe him that.'

I felt myself wreckage, marooned by the tide. Inert, yet certain now that there was worse to come. What else, what more had Jean-Claude promised to Ahmed?

I was frightened alone in the cottage. I was frightened that I was not alone, that there was a presence hiding in the air. I felt under observation, as I had when the doe stared. It was Montaine, I was sure of it. She had been pursuing me. Now that I was defenceless, she was closing in. I felt a sort of agony: my own and hers.

I had thought Jean-Claude's and mine was that 'perfect love that casteth out fear' . . . I never imagined it would leave room for feelings of resentment and indifference. I asked myself why Jean-Claude left me in the dark. I asked myself what I would feel if on his journey back to Paris he had an accident. Did I mind that he had been torn from his work and from me – by Ahmed, his dead sister's devastated amour? Did I feel sad for the sadness he endured? Was his sadness tinged with guilt? I wondered. I found that I no longer felt for Jean-Claude but for myself. I had lost the sense of being part of another. I had heard the

161

bell toll . . . the wave of ecstasy which drove me on to this shore had pressed me into a dark, dull interior. I was in exile.

Otto said that we all gravitate towards what it is we want. But he never explained how it is that we can so easily be led by involuntary desire. And I knew all too well that we possess our lover only in our minds, that passionate love is incompatible with life.

I could not follow my routine. It was senseless without Jean-Claude. I was not hungry and the rooms did not seem to deserve cleanliness and embellishment in his absence. I felt an impulse to flee from the cottage in the early morning and stay out of it until dusk. I felt under constant, persistent threat. When I did return, I locked myself in and heaved the great oak table against the door and fastened the windows.

I did not dare walk in the forest or the field. And so I wandered over to the farm. In the corner of the yard I saw Mme Deloche's great-aunt seated on a bench, her long skirt trailing in the dirt. She had a chicken in her lap. She was twisting its neck. Round and round she twisted. The animal was screeching and flapping the air. The old peasant was demonic in her rage. As I turned the corner, chicken and peasant grew limp together, one in triumph, the other in defeat. Shaken, I fled down the lane towards the village. And then I slowed down again. I wandered from the wheelwright to the harness-maker and the basket-weaver before entering the café. I felt a huge emptiness in which I feared to be dissolved. A torpor held me fast in its strait-jacket. I could not shake free of it. I was feeling remote. I wondered why, but as I wondered the subject faded, my mind wandered . . . I lost myself. I tried to focus on my interior but there was nothing to focus on: just space, disappearing into further emptiness.

A feeling of terror mounted in me, and I dragged myself to the telephone and rang Émile. It was as if a voice not my own was making the call. I confided nothing of my circumstances, merely asked Émile how he was and kept him telling me at length, without interrupting him. I wanted the call to go on endlessly. He urged me to take a day off and visit him. He kept insisting. I was pleased by that. I said I would bear his suggestion in mind. At least there was someone at the end of a line who knew me.

Every day that passed while Jean-Claude was away I became increasingly disorientated. I feared I was going mad. The person who was putting one step in front of the other across the field to the lane was not me, somehow. What was I doing here, alone? And why? Where was this self that had gone missing? Did I have no control over anything? Only questions presented themselves. Questions and more questions. Every one intractable.

I reached the square and went and sat in the Café des Chasseurs, where men with nowhere to rush sat smoking and drinking, blank-faced.

M. Deloche was there with a stranger. The two approached sluggishly with their glasses and sat down at my table. Suddenly, M. Deloche took leave of his friend. He said he had to conduct some business with the grain merchant. I found myself alone with a man the skin of whose face had the texture of hide, tanned the colour of stout. In the normal way I would not have followed him into the gunsmith's, a place of such absolute masculinity, smelling of game and metal, ringing with men's talk. But these were not normal times for me. I was a player in a drama written and cast by Jean-Claude, who had not rehearsed me for it. I was hungry for company. The man talked non-stop and did not expect me to contribute. He told me he had been a sailor, had known the bitter odour of disease and been a casualty in the wars of the elements, but nothing had been as dire as the loss of his woman to another. 'I had to get away,' he confided through gravel. 'I took to the vice ports in revenge.'

Images of animals huddled together for warmth, safety and companionship floated into my mind as I stood at the side of this man, watching him examine firearms. As he moved along the rows of guns, his wooden leg sounded dull thuds. When he opened his acrid mouth he displayed broken and missing teeth. I wondered at his beard: was it infested? It was hard to imagine he had known romance – and still had it in mind.

'And now I am back to claim her!' Triumphantly,

he slapped a wodge of notes down on the polished mahogany counter, as if anxious to be rid of it, and snatching a 12 bore from the gunsmith, he strode out into the square.

The breach that separated me from my past gaped open. Over the wide divide I could not recall who I had once been. Suddenly, without history, I felt transient.

I never have properly recalled how I had spent the larger part of my time in Préfleur when Jean-Claude was away. Had someone insisted he had seen me in Romorantin, or further afield, I should not have been able to confirm or deny the sighting. But I don't remember having ventured further than the village. Only sensation survived: being deafened by the rooster, yet finding silence unendurable. Being irredeemably bored, yet unable to concentrate enough to read. There was nothing I felt inclined to do, no action I wished to take. I had no dream. I was indifferent to anything outside myself, and I was conscious of not being prepared to live entirely in the mind.

I was confused. 'If there were no mirrors,' someone once said, 'we might look more closely at ourselves.' There was no mirror in the cottage but I did not know where or how to look. I had no proper memory of the deep past, and no sense of the future. The merest action I managed to take seemed infinitely long in completing. For example, I might butter a piece of bread and be unable to gauge whether the procedure was taking me seconds or days. I did observe myself: I spied on myself; every step I took I counted. But I did not come close to any but my outward gestures.

One night in bed I thought I heard knocking at the cottage door. Supposing it was Montaine? She knows I am alone and vulnerable. Should I let her in? She must have come from very far . . . be tired and hungry . . . her shoes worn thin . . . sand and stones embedded in the soles of her feet. She wants Jean-Claude back. She wants me to release him . . . I rise and lean out of the window into the dark. The branch of the walnut tree is striking the cottage as rhythmically as an oar striking the river.

I do not sense my body. I do not remember my name. I am suspended in anonymity, lying weight-less, displacing a mere wisp of atmosphere. Not knowing where I am, I cannot be sure who I am. I defrost slowly. I become aware of hands – huge flappers with tiny bulges on long branches. My self is a speck at the centre of uncontrollable limbs stretching into the void. Within my dreaming head swims the small, wild cat at the end of Aunt Florence's garden, Mother fastening her garnet necklace in the path of a passing horseman raising dust, and the repeated refrain 'Even the weariest river winds somewhere safe to sea' . . . And then a great wave breaks over me and I emerge into full consciousness. It is morning. It is desolation. The lonely cannot enjoy solitude. I stood thinking at the door. I felt I had forgotten something but could not remember what.

Jean-Claude returned from Paris mute and exhausted, as if under a spell. I left him as usual to work in peace all day, certain that his reproachful silence which accompanied our mealtimes would lift at night. He reverted to the habits of our early days: those of an infant. I consoled him at my breast when he wept. I gave him my fingers to suck. I did not question him because I knew he would be unable to describe what and how he felt, even if he had been willing to do so. Nor did I complain when he kept me awake, twisting and turning, sighing and moaning. He needed me to know and take on his sorrow, and find solutions. He needed me as unction to soothe his pain. I spread myself liberally – or so I thought. I felt protective. Sometimes, when I made a move towards the cottage door, as if to leave on some errand, he called me back. He was frightened to be alone.

Little by little he dropped hints, but no details. He railed against Otto: Otto had money; Otto could help Ahmed find somewhere decent to live . . . get him detoxified . . . get him papers. Otto owed this to Jean-Claude. But Otto was a Jew, bad at paying debts. Maman had always warned: 'You'll get nothing from that quarter!'

'But you have!' I said. 'Frequently! Otto's been a good friend to you over the years.'

'And me? What have I been to him?'

I hated the way he laughed.

Jean-Claude's anti-Semitism was an eternally smouldering fire upon which, when memory served, he threw kerosene to create a blaze. It was a habit with him. A mechanical response with which he had grown up, natural as breathing. I wondered how it came to pass that a thinking man bore the prejudices of his unthinking parents into the future? The Guérignys were simple people, as fearful of strangers on their land as they were of foxes. Foxes took off with their chickens and rabbits; Jews with their profits.

I was never to learn the full range of Mme Guérigny's bigotry. I assumed she subscribed to that of her kin. (Her unexpected acceptance of North Africans – Nissim, for instance – was explained by Montaine's example.) She used to repeat the expression *on attend pas mieux*, through tight lips, in relation to any misdemeanour reported to have been committed by a Jew. What might a God-fearing Catholic expect from those whose ancestors murdered Christ and who, to this day, drank the blood of innocent Christian babies? I did ask Mme Guérigny what evidence she had for these sacrificial murders. She did not need evidence, she assured me, it was a well-known fact. Another well-known fact was that all that stuff about the concentration camps was a gross exaggeration. ('There were no gas chambers. It was a hoax.') It had to be or how was it that all the banks, shops, factories and insurance companies were still in the hands of Jews?

'Madame,' I tried, 'I must insist: what you say is not true!'

'Oh, you only object . . . you only defend the Jews because your husband is a Jew. But I notice, little madam, you were pleased enough to find yourself a good Catholic . . .' And she sniffed. 'Jews may be welcome in England, but they are not welcome here. I am told,' and here she became confidential, 'many among them are perverts!'

Ça c'est riche! I thought to myself, and almost smiled.

'And there are revolutionaries among them. They have no roots, they are bound to another land. They are immigrants who travel across the world breaking down the moral order, bringing chaos to organized society. We don't need change. We don't like change.'

I watched her inhale deeply, her ample bosom proving like dough.

There was no point in attempting to educate Mme Guérigny. But her words were Jean-Claude's and he wanted me to think his thoughts. The implications were too horrible. I felt uncomfortably compromised.

'I find your anti-Semitism absolutely disgusting!' I managed, as he slumped down at table to eat. I was surprised by the vehemence in my own voice. However, just behind the vacant expression he offered me, I detected fear. I realized then just how many times, over the months, I had had evidence of this fear, and how careful I had always been to avoid doing or saying anything that could threaten the bastions he erected to guard his frail defences. But now I was ready to put his vulnerability behind me and consider things objectively.

I was, after all, living with a man who was stealing from me, keeping part of his life secret from me, who expected me to adapt myself to his obsessive timekeeping.

'On mange ou on mange pas? Remues-toi!'

Never was a man so constrained by time. He performed everything to the clock. It was as if an ill-timed or ill-executed gesture on his part and his world would collapse. At first the disappearance of my little *objets d'art*, my lavish art books and pieces of jewellery did not bother me. I was so in love with Jean-Claude! But I did wonder, after a year or more, how it was that he and Mme G expected me to use the public baths rather than offer me the convenience of the bathroom in the *pavillon*. These matters had a sort of equivalence in my mind: I had my possessions to offer Jean-Claude, his mother had her bathroom to offer me . . . But it was not to be. And there was the business of the motor cycle.

When we came to Préfleur I asked Jean-Claude if he would teach me to drive the motor cycle. It would be a help if I could get about the country-side when he was working. No, he said, he would not. 'I maintain the machine. I drive it.' And that was that. Final. Not open to discussion.

I regarded this at first as meanness. Later, I saw it was part of his fear: if I had the means to escape, perhaps I would use it? If I entered the *pavillon* alone, for such an intimate matter as bathing, perhaps I would occupy space reserved for Montaine?

Jean-Claude expected me to respect all his fads – especially the fuss and nonsense about the particular brand of coffee-beans he must have, and how he had to grind them himself, give the machine at least one hundred turns, sit comfortably. When first I met him, this ritual had seemed stylish to me. It was not very long before I came to see it as simply one fad among others. Almost as if without one or two eccentricities he would feel characterless.

And there was something costive about his secretiveness. Not having been associated with people with his range of peculiarities, I wondered whether they were the materials of his prejudices.

After the initial shock I felt in Théovard, I came to regard Jean-Claude's relations with Otto in much the same light as mine with Émile. Both of us were giving ourselves in the service of a third party. Jean-Claude – unable to support Ahmed himself, even with the money he raised from the sale of my belongings – wanted Otto to support him. And I wanted Émile to support Jean-Claude. I had noticed that a great deal of moral indignation was wasted in England over matters relating to sexual encounters. That, I concluded, was because, by comparison with the French, the English were a joyless lot and confined sex to the obligations of the marriage bed. I could not make up my mind which was cause and which effect. In my experience, the marriage bed was uncomfortable, even distasteful, and invariably boring, whereas sex with my lover had been a revelation. And there was nothing to connect the nights I shared with Jean-Claude with the afternoons I spent with Émile. However, all relations should be conducted with kindness and generosity. I did not approve of Jean-Claude's displays of impatient bigotry with Otto, from whom he wanted an instantaneous return. I was careful not to be as blatant with Émile. At first I thought it ironic that Jean-Claude had chosen a Jewish friend to use. But on reflection I understood that this was no coincidence: Jean-Claude needed a Jew with whom to debase himself in order to have the licence to abuse him in return. No one else attracted such vituperation from him. But his anti-Semitism, although a powerful obsession, was one among many obsessions that governed his life.

'No one likes Jews, Opal. They are too ugly, too rich, too powerful . . .' While I wondered about his motives, he stoked up his contempt for the whole Jewish race, which had not had the decency to get itself wiped out, as rumoured. 'You believe all that, *ma pauvre?* . . . You'd believe anything. It's all lies . . . the camps . . . the gas chambers.

It's a publicity stunt to gain sympathy. They know it's sympathy they need. They're not stupid. That's one thing you can say for the Jews: they're not stupid!'

I felt mounting contempt for Jean-Claude. I felt my lip curl, and the inside of my mouth dry out and tighten as if I had been sucking lemons. With the increasing irritation I was feeling for my lover, I was faced with the realization that the early promise of happiness infinitely extended was dramatically receding. I saw why it was receding. At first, I closed my ears to what I did not want to hear. I registered that it was Mme Guérigny and her brothers and sisters-in-law who uttered the calumnies, and only later that Jean-Claude never took issue with them. Indeed, it was he who, returning to the Sunday lunch-table after taking a telephone call from Otto, referred to the *sale juif*. And it was I who, objecting, and saying 'Otto's a very decent man', was made to sound priggish, so that when the word 'decent' echoed in my mind, I thought back to Théovard and felt confused.

When I met Jean-Claude I found something in his face, his speech and gestures, that alerted my heart and made it a gift to him. He described a life so different from my own that I could not have imagined it – 'She loved me for the dangers I had passed, and I loved her, that she did pity them.' One in which, on a single day, he could have been rounded up at bayonet-point or celebrated a cigarette. His security had been in a family that was to lose its roots, and in a sister who was to lose her life. Because he discovered something of his sister in me, he was determined to 'save' me. It must have been a continual jolt when I reacted to things differently from Montaine.

'She was never still for long. Her goal was not to rest,' he said sadly, finding me lying on the sofa with a book. I caught the ironies but did not budge. 'She was always singing, joking . . .' I detected his disappointment. But I knew it was useless to try to make up for all his losses. 'She could never return Ahmed's love. She had no more to give, once she had emptied her heart to me.' There! The secret was out. So, too, the source of Jean-Claude's guilt and his outstanding debt to Ahmed. 'She was a thoughtful soul. She considered most carefully whether life was or was not worth living before she killed herself. I think her decision was courageous. She loved herself enough not to permit herself to go on suffering, and she loved me more than life. She couldn't give herself to Ahmed and couldn't keep herself for me, you understand.' He sat down on the floor and, taking my hand in his, curled his fingers like bindweed around mine. 'And I go on working on my memorials to her, to gather the strength to write more . . . Those who know how to listen, will find my whole life embedded there.'

It was later that evening that he took a white muslin dress out of the bag with which he had returned from Paris and asked me to wear it as a nightdress. I was startled. How insidious was Montaine's part in my role in Jean-Claude's drama! He was not setting in motion the puppets of the past to destroy them. He was reactivating them for life. But I gave in. I let him sleep that night – and succeeding nights – with Montaine . . .

Everything in Jean-Claude's life had been decided before he met me, and I was being fitted into a preordained pattern. He may well have imagined when he met me that he was acquiring the means of escape from the kingdom of the past. In the event, he made me captive there, and closed impenetrable bars about himself. He confused his childhood adventure with that of his hero, Meaulnes. It seemed that he came to associate his love affair with me with the one Meaulnes had with Valentine – and Meaulnes's resultant guilt and loss of purity. Nostalgia for secret quests, obsessions, purity, past promises to keep at the expense of present obligations, these should be confined to the realm of fiction, I thought. Jean-Claude was inspired to compose by loss; but because his desire for the past was stronger than his need for fulfilment in the present, his life and work were continually on the brink of dissolution.

'The party is over!' Again and again the little tune Jean-Claude had composed for Frantz's words turned in my head. And I heard how the music acquired a force his understanding lacked. But I was not going to submit to the suffering of being preserved in a past that was not my own. I did not want to share the rest of my life with a ghost. Eventually, if Jean-Claude wished to go on living with death and the dead, he would have to do so alone. He had taken me on to smooth his path, and this I had done. But I was not prepared to drive new roads across continents. Not now!

PARIS AND LONDON

I went to the bird market and bought a songbird for you my love.
I went to the flower market and bought flowers for you, my love.
I went to the iron merchant and I bought chains, heavy chains for you, my love.
And then I went to the slave market and sought you.
But I did not find you, my love.

Jacques Prevert

During the last few weeks we were in Préfleur we spoke little. Jean-Claude finished his opera *Meaulnes*. I almost completed *Cooking with Difficulty*. I do not believe Jean-Claude's feelings towards me had changed – mine towards him had. Or perhaps it was not so much my feelings that had changed as my thoughts.

I should have known that Jean-Claude would wish to return to Paris a few days prior to the anniversary of Montaine's death, a date embossed not only on his and Mme Guérigny's mind but on my own. The previous year, he had left the attic at 8 a.m. and had not returned until after 11 p.m., having failed to tell me that he was intending to spend the day with Maman, and why. It was evident that the ever-present shadow which fell across the lives of Mme Guérigny and her son had never been darker. I did not ask if they had visited Montaine's grave, or if others who had loved Montaine had joined them. Nor was I informed.

It had been raining. The rain had left the

boulevards lacquered, and the sky calm as death. Jean-Claude rode slowly between the rows of pollarded limes and lofty planes, the sound of the crowd drowned in the swell of the traffic. I was conscious of the silence of the past year. I had time to scrutinize the benches occupied by beggars and their bundles, and to watch the children playing in the little squares bounded by green iron railings, to envy gross matrons and their lapdogs trotting between the *pâtissière* and the *charcuterie* . . . women in aprons washing the pavements, standing back to let pedestrians pass. I looked up at the jumble of rooftops with their abundance of chimney-pots, the florid iron balconies at the dormer windows. *Teinturie, Laverie, Blanchisserie* . . . The whole of beautiful Paris, cold and indifferent to me, seemed to mock me. It was holding a party to which I had not been invited. I felt leaden.

Jean-Claude had been back to Reine twice during the year, to visit his mother. He had made the round trip in a day. He rang her regularly from the café or the post office and urged her to come and stay with us. He had sent her postcards – never a letter, that would have wasted working time. She did not reply to his cards, and when she spoke to him on the telephone he said she always declined his invitations firmly. I was glad of this; I should have made every effort to see to her comfort in the cottage but I could imagine the thunderous impact that Préfleur would have on her. It would have been an unnecessary and cruel blow for her to see her old home in its state of decay. She would have been tempted to visit all of Montaine's old haunts. Everything would have combined to emphasize the fact that she was no longer part of the terrain her ancestors had occupied for so many generations. Like death itself, a removal can be a complete loss. I did not want her to face the rings that dissolve into the banks of time's pond when the dead-weight falls to its depths. I asked Jean-Claude how his mother sounded on the telephone.

'No more unhappy, no less unhappy . . .' Nothing could pierce the aura of her grief or interrupt her preoccupation with mourning. 'The cow grows hoarse, weeping for her calf . . .'

At times when I sensed that the gulf between Jean-Claude and me was so wide as to be almost unbridgeable, I would wonder how it was that our love-making had lost nothing of its fervour. We still behaved as if to sleep were a waste of time. It was not for some years after we had separated that I had to face the fact that the deepest part of one's being is always inaccessible to another, and that only when we are lost in passion, eager above all else for our own gratification – yet unconscious that this is the case – that we ignore the gulf, forget that we are strangers. That part of me which, when first we met, I should willingly have made over to Jean-Claude – and which he seemed to make no attempt to acquire – was, of course, no more available to him than the source of his being was to me. Only in our passion did this not suggest itself to me as mean retention on his part. It was because we were strangers in bed that we were passionately involved there. Out of bed, in a companionship reliant upon my entering his fantasy world and behaving as if it were real, we did less well, eventually. I would not – could not – rake over the embers of his past with him persistently. At first, desire had engendered belief. Now, I felt myself drying up, burning with a slow flame and, like a piece of paper, crumbling to dust when he sought to ignite my interest.

I was sick, too, of death – this family member. Mme Guérigny admitted to me shortly after our return that she was feeling a certain contentment in being one year nearer joining her daughter. I could understand how she felt; I realized that anyone who convinced herself that, when she took the holy biscuit she was uniting herself with God, would find it easy to convince herself that in death she would be united with her daughter. But I could no longer bear my life to be shrouded in the Guérigny grief. I was young. I had years ahead of me. I did not cleave to their affectation that man's essential role is to endure the sufferings of a senseless existence until death provides the bounty of eternal life.

I don't know if it ever occurred to me to regret my inability to have a child by Jean-Claude. Both he and Mme Guérigny made it clear that, so far as they were concerned, the family had reached completion; it had been torn asunder, and would integrate on Jean-Claude's death. Since life was a vale of tears, I imagine his death was also an event to which they both looked forward, impatiently. Perhaps something of Mme G's tolerance of my relationship with her son was due to her knowing that I was barren. This was no place for me to linger. I was going to put down roots, achieve something, give meaning to my existence. Without meaning there is only suffering, and I was not going to leave it at that. I had started to fear that each of us controls the manner in which we die much more closely than is generally supposed. Our lives manifest the ends appropriate to them. I was not condemned to the Guérignys' life sentence.

The leaden feeling that weighed heavily on me as Jean-Claude rode into Paris did not lift when we fetched up at the house in the rue Victorie. I knew that instead of returning – as I had hoped, a year ago – to easier times ahead, with the opera scheduled for transmission and further commissions being made on its back, more diffficult times were ahead. Émile was going to revenge himself on Jean-Claude for what he regarded as his arrogance.

I determined I would not be the one to break the news to Jean-Claude that, despite his protestations, his opera would *never* be broadcast – that the law protected Xavier Frontenac. But I wondered how to arrange things so that Émile Chaillot told him. I suggested as gently as I could to Jean-Claude that he give Chaillot a ring. No, he said – and he was defiant – there was no need. He had completed the commission, rather more fully than had been envisaged, and all that was required of him now was to deliver it.

'I shall be going into the city tomorrow. I have some people to see. I'll deliver it to the radio in the afternoon.'

I was not going to be left in Reine to attend to the chores. I told Jean-Claude to drop me off at the Place St Michel. I rang Otto on the off-chance. And before meeting him, I wandered about the Left Bank reminding myself that I had been prescribed the city of love to feast my senses.

'How's Jean-Claude?'

'Depressed. Drained of energy – and purpose, for that matter. He knows without admitting it to himself that the Radio's not going to transmit the opera. Chaillot is going to ask for the advance back.'

'Oh dear! Shall I have a word with him?'

'That's kind of you, Otto, but there's really no point. The rights are not his to dispose of. Jean-Claude knew from the start what the position was. He was asked to do the *music* for *Frontenac's* libretto . . .'

I did not need to go on about Jean-Claude's obstinacy, foolishness and arrogance. Otto understood from my tone what I felt, and despite his positive feeling for Jean-Claude, he knew his faults. He did say that he thought the future might be difficult for us. 'He lacks prudence,' he admitted.

Otto was an emotional nomad. Because of his position *vis-a-vis* me – friend of Helmut, lover of Jean-Claude – I could never tell whether he was frank with me. I had found him somewhat ingratiating. That was understandable. He had a peculiar habit of sliding effortlessly from throwing me a bait to hitting me over the head with it.

'I have observed he has been behaving a mite more realistically since he's had you in his life, my dear . . . I wonder what it is that intervenes to make him so self-destructive?'

'His happiness is connected with desire, not fulfilment,' I explained.

Otto did not pursue this observation. He said I had probably done all I could (little did he know), but that no one was omnipotent and I should not try to be for Jean-Claude what Maman had been – and still was, to some extent. 'He'll give you one hell of a time if you persist. He's bound in an oedipal grapple.'

We were sitting in the Lipp. Otto had ordered Alsatian beer, sausages and sauerkraut for two. Once his tongue was loosened, I knew I was going to be told more than I wanted to know about

185

Jean-Claude's past. I could tell that Otto's face expressed more sympathy than he felt. I felt insulted; Otto was confiding information about Jean-Claude to me. He was overlooking the fact that I had been living with Jean-Claude for more than three years. He started by saying that after Montaine's death Jean-Claude had survived in the dark – a dirty, torn piece of sacking over the window and newspaper plugging the broken panes, obscuring the merest ray of sunlight. I did not interrupt. I did not remind him that it was I who had replaced the newspaper with mended panes and the sacking with curtains. I wondered why Jean-Claude had not mentioned it to him. He went on to describe how Jean-Claude had starved himself, how much weight he had lost and in what condition were the nerves he wore on his sleeve. I let him talk on. I knew there would be some details that might fill in a few gaps and, indeed, I had not known that Mme G had kept in touch with Otto and that, prior to my arrival on the scene, he frequently drove over to Reine with tempting delicacies that Jean-Claude invariably refused to eat. Poor Madame, I thought, how deeply she must resent my usurping her place.

Otto must have talked to me for hours that day. I felt he was vying with me for proprietary rights over Jean-Claude. Part of me did not care one bit. I remember how he described the messages Mme Guérigny maintained she received from Montaine. She used to ring Otto at his office, rather as if she felt this experience had some professional interest to Otto.

'The messages were nothing more than trivial fragments, like matters overheard in the Métro, poor woman . . . I never discussed them with Jean-Claude and I don't know if she did. I used to try and get him out into the country in the car. I wanted to get him down to Théovard. But he had been there with Montaine and he couldn't bear to see the place again – not then. I was astonished that he agreed to come down with you. And even more astonished he went back to la Sologne – not just physically but emotionally. What a boon you are to him, Opal, my dear. And what a pity *Meaulnes* will never be broadcast.'

A pity!

'Madame used to stand at the gate to the *pavillon*, looking down the lane into the rue Victorie, in the belief that Montaine's absence could be accounted for. "She's taking the long way back," she would say, "the sun's still warm . . . she's enjoying herself . . . she's forgotten the time . . ." And Jean-Claude would connive in this. "Montaine's gone missing. Many went missing during the war. Many turned up again. Eventually." Poor woman. She could never accept that her God is more concerned with his apples than his children.'

It was difficult for me to put myself in the Guérigny frame of mind, to accommodate both the knowledge of a beloved's death and the sense of her imminent return. I, too, had seen what I

187

believed I saw and heard; what I wanted to hear. But now I no longer did. I knew that such contradictions could be resolved for Jean-Claude in his work, and I felt that he, like me, should not allow them to dominate life.

Otto confessed that Jean-Claude stole from him. He was ashamed to admit it to me, and I understood why. He even sought to excuse his friend on the grounds of his poverty. I did not confide to Otto that Jean-Claude was stealing from me. I, too, felt guilty for never having known poverty. I asked Otto if he knew about Jean-Claude's contempt for the law. I told him how he had put up a man who was *interdit de séjour* . . .

'Like everything else about Jean-Claude, one has to go back to his roots in la Sologne. He betrayed a Jewish family to save his own skin.' It was impossible to tell from Otto's tone of voice how he felt about this. I searched his face, but it too was controlled. 'But the war was a different country, Opal. People were driven to their limits. They behaved with both unimaginable courage and contemptible cowardice. They exposed strengths and weaknesses they didn't know were theirs. You have to ask yourself how you think you would have done in their place. Today, his anti-Semitism has become a habit, a mechanical response, a focus for all his resentments: his poverty, his lack of formal education, his peripheral place in the world of music . . . I have to say, I feel nothing but pity for him. Mark my words, he feels as guilty as all hell for what he did, which explains the verbal abuse. I tease him about his prejudice. It shuts him up for the time being, and I'm not going to give him the satisfaction of thinking his insolence cuts any ice with me. I'm not going to dignify his abuse by reacting to it seriously. It's a pose with him, to some extent. He attaches himself to his peasant roots by blaming the Jews.'

Was this pure candour? I asked myself. Or was Otto's summary dismissal of his friend's insults something to do with his feeling himself of greater social and intellectual consequence than Jean-Claude? But then he murmured half under his breath something to the effect that 'the boy had cost him much suffering'.

I had wanted to ask Otto if he thought Jean-Claude's anti-Semitism, his lawlessness and his stealing were linked. Was it because everything that had been precious to him had been torn from him that he had to find someone to blame for his losses; someone to take advantage of, someone from whom he could derive consolation? Was this his idea of conquering fate? But I desisted. I could not pursue a conversation that would put me in the degrading position of having to ask Otto to fill in further gaps in my knowledge and understanding of my own lover.

I accompanied Otto back to his office. I wanted to revisit the place where I had first caught sight of Jean-Claude years ago. While I stood surveying the scene, Otto watched me.

'There's something different about you, Opal. I can't put my finger on it, but you've changed.

'Perhaps it's the innocent expression that's faded.'

Inside, I felt myself smile.

There was no way that Émile could get in contact with me without Jean-Claude's knowledge, and there was no legitimate excuse for him to do so openly. He had sent the contract for the 'Chansons de Mani' by post to Préfleur. Jean-Claude signed it and returned to Paris, to find a cheque waiting for him. And then the row broke out over *Meaulnes*. Jean-Claude delivered the score; Émile Chaillot returned it. Furious telephone conversations between the two ensued. Jean-Claude may have had artistic integrity on his side but he did not have a legal leg to stand on. The situation brought out the viciousness in him, and I felt he was almost certainly going to alienate Émile for good.

And so I was extremely surprised when no more than weeks later Émile telephoned Jean-Claude and proposed to him the idea that he should take up an appointment as composer-in-residence at an American university. Someone had had to drop out at the last minute and there was an unexpected vacancy to be filled. The university was in Georgia. The appointment was for six months. He would not be required to lecture. He would be free to pursue his own work, but must make himself available to students of composition. I was stunned when Jean-Claude repeated this proposal to me. At first I thought how generous it was of Émile to bother about Jean-Claude at all. But then I started to wonder whether the explanation was not to be found elsewhere. Was Émile engineering a way of getting my lover out of his way and making me free for himself?

The opportunity to escape from Reine appealed to Jean-Claude, even though he had been back for only a few weeks. He had quickly re-established his old routine of working all day in the attic and going out occasionally at night to meet anonymous friends. He referred to himself as *le prisonnier*. Suddenly he saw a gap in his prison bars and some light. He would enjoy being comfortably housed, having a music room with a Steinway grand, and an orchestra, however inexperienced, on tap to play his compositions, the largest part of which he had never heard. He spoke dreamily of the riches of America, the possibilities for his music, the one-in-the-eye for those with whom he felt himself continuously in competition. And then he pointed out that he would need me to translate for him with students and the authorities. What a good thing he had me! I answered at once that I hardly imagined such an arrangement would be acceptable. 'The appointment is for one – for a composer . . .' He ignored me.

I am not sure if I ever took the idea of America very seriously. I think I must have realized that Jean-Claude had neither the nerve nor the genuine confidence to take up an appointment in a language he did not speak. Nevertheless, he went and discussed the details of the job with the cultural attaché at the US Embassy.

There was more than one reason why I could not accompany Jean-Claude to America. The more I repeated those I was willing to talk about, the more determined he was to accept the job. I could see how attractive was the chance it offered him to leave Reine, and he deserved it. I also understood, from little hints dropped here and there, that he wanted to get out of the country while his music was starting to impinge on the public. For despite the disaster of the opera, a backlog of his work was now being performed. Critics sickened him. Parasites! Blood-sucking little crawling creatures . . . they pandered either to popular taste or to a current fad. He might be going to become a fad. 'They come and go, fads, you know . . . They don't have the slightest understanding of what I'm trying to do.'

I could not tell whether this was a reasonable assessment or whether it was neurotic. And when a half-page profile of Jean-Claude appeared in *Le Nouvel Observateur* I really could not make up my mind whether he was more genuinely displeased than pleased. The piece hinted at 'a difficult war' and made much of personal loss, which lent a certain 'haunting melancholy' to his work. Was it this kind of intrusion that made Jean-Claude anxious? Or was it that expectations were being aroused which he did not know if he could meet? All he said was that he did not want anyone 'fishing about' in his private life.

Of course he did not know how it was the piece in the *Nouvel Observateur* had come to be written. I did, but could not tell him. Émile Chaillot told me that he had telephoned the writer and spoken to him for a good seven minutes about what was going on in the music world. He had flattered him; had said he always read his critiques with particular care and was stimulated by his musical acumen and pellucid expression – 'The sort of things critics like to hear of themselves . . .' And he had dined the man at his favourite restaurant. The profile appeared ten days after the dinner under the rubric 'There is heard her voice in all his music'.

Sheafs of documents arrived from Georgia and from the US Embassy.

'You'll have to sign this!' Jean-Claude said, handing me an affidavit, to swear I was his wife. 'We'll have to go to the *notaire.*'

'I can't swear to being your wife. I'm not. I'm Helmut's.'

'But if you don't sign, you won't get a free passage and I won't get an allowance for you.'

'I can't perjure myself.'

'Oh my God, Opal, you're so English!'

The fact was that for a single man the job offered

almost half the sum allotted to a couple. In addition, whereas Jean-Claude would get his passage paid by the university, as a mere 'friend' I should have to pay my own. I did not have the ready money for this, nor did he.

'You don't want to go, do you?'

In fact, I did not. But it was for a reason that would cut no ice with Jean-Claude and so I did not put it to him. I simply said that if I had the money and was able to pay my fare and support myself in America, I would accompany him. Since I hadn't and couldn't, there was no question of my going.

For the first time, we had a row that went on for days. I had never experienced his obduracy before or, if I had, had identified it as something else. Now he dug his heels in: America was a place of infinite possibilities where an artist with no money and no background could gain recognition in a big way. It was a chance in a million, and if he did not grasp it, one of his competitors would. And it was I who stood in his way – I, who professed to want his success as much as he . . .

'Go on your own,' I suggested. But it was disingenuous of me. I knew he would never take on students in a language he did not speak. He had to have me there to interpret. Furthermore, he needed someone who understood his way of working, and his goals. I was ruining his chances of getting free from the chains of misery attaching him to a rotten *banlieue de Paris*.

It was true that I would never perjure myself. However, my reason for not attempting to make plans to go to Georgia had nothing much to do with the appointment under discussion. If the university had been, say, in Vermont, I would have agreed to go and would somehow have found the money to pay my fare and support myself in America – and interpret for Jean-Claude. The reason I would not go and live there for six days, let alone six months, was segregation. Georgia was the South.

Mme Guérigny brought the Sunday lunch ritual to a close as soon as she had buried M. Guérigny. I was puzzled by her timing. Surely, I thought, she would need to have her brothers and their wives around her more, not less, frequently now? But it was not the case. Once in a while she allowed Gaston or Marius to drive over to Reine and take her back to one or other of their houses for Sunday lunch. But she confided to Jean-Claude that this was a concession wrung from her to avoid argument: not something she had initiated, or enjoyed.

One Sunday morning, when I was looking out of the window, I saw Mme Guérigny leave church and walk from the rue de Fleuve along the rue Victorie towards Bluot's, and return with a box nicely wrapped and tied with gold string. Bluot's baked lavish cakes for saints' days, Easter and Sundays. During the week their more humble *petits pains au chocolat, brioches* and *palmiers* were consigned to greaseproof bags. I wondered who was going to tea at the *pavillon*.

It was mid-afternoon when we heard Mme Guérigny's strident market voice shouting from the courtyard up to out window, asking us to come over.

Entering the *pavillon* with only Mme Guérigny in residence was a deeply depressing experience. The place was cold, as usual, but now the odours were all stale, and I noticed a pervading disorder. I wondered why she wanted us both. I imagined it was to occupy her in her loneliness. Perhaps she envisaged a more general conversation than what she shared with Jean-Claude. I was entirely wrong. Mme Guérigny wanted to persuade me to accompany Jean-Claude to America. It was her duty to tell me – a 'mother's duty' – that my obstinate refusal to comply with Jean-Claude's wishes meant I was becoming a burden to him. 'An artist – and he is sensitive – must have continual support. His wife or companion, whatever the case, must be utterly unselfish.' And she outlined the role of an artist's companion as she saw it. Unsurprisingly, it confined itself largely to the home – to the space between the sink and the bed. However, it also called for the typing of letters, the negotiating of contracts and the entertaining of the 'right' people. I smiled to myself. 'Above all, you must put Jean-Claude's needs before your own.' I reassured Mme Guérigny that her son's and my interests were one.

It amused me to think back to my life in London. There I had had the right to follow my own devices throughout the day. I was expected home for my husband only in the evenings.

'Your friend, Monsieur von Kramitz, wouldn't he help?' Mme Guérigny shouted to Jean-Claude who, for one reason or another, had found it preferable to escape into the bathroom and shut the door.

'Why should he?' I asked.

'He's rich, that's why. And he's fond of Jean-Claude, he's always on the telephone . . . He thinks very highly of his work . . . What about Otto . . . ?' she started when Jean-Claude walked back into the kitchen.

'I'm not sure,' he mumbled.

'Well, one thing's for sure, if there's going to be another saviour it won't be a Jew!' And she thumped the cake down so hard in front of me that I expected the plate to shatter.

I thought over her remark and why she had made it. I realized that she – and possibly Jean-Claude – might be expecting me to approach Helmut for the money.

'Maman's fiercely protective . . . and now all she has to protect is me.' He was trying to put me off the scent, perhaps, trying to explain, trying to seem reasonable.

'You see' (I would explain, I would be reasonable), 'even if I were willing to perjure myself, I'd never get away with it. I'd be bound to be found out in the end. There'd be the most awful dust-up. I'd have my passport confiscated. I'd be fined. I might even be sent to prison. And you'd lose the job. And you'd have an awful lot of explaining to do ever after.' But I could see I had lost his attention. All I said simply slid off the shell into which he retreated when confronted by words he did not want to hear.

Our relationship had formed itself by an aggregation of layers. At the most profound, over which we had no conscious control, we were ideally suited and at peace. Had we been animals we would have hunted co-operatively, bred regularly and protected one another rigorously. At an effective level, the one at which I made it possible for Jean-Claude to work uninterruptedly, I felt both the benefits of a companionable relationship with someone of whom I was, in many ways, admiring, and a sense of my own worth: I was useful to him. I did not mind the inconveniences of the attic. I did not crave a more sociable life. I had had enough of luxury and distractions with Helmut. I was accustomed to my own company; after Mother died I was alone in the house with Father, and he was seldom at home. When I married, I left behind the few friends of my childhood, and made no lasting friends in London. Once I got to France, Jean-Claude was the only company I wanted to keep. It was as if I had 'come home' to something familiar.

However, at a surface level I faced diffficulties.

Jean-Claude had a different way of looking at moral issues from the one in which I had been brought up, and judged correct. For one thing, he was comfortable with theft. For another, he despised the Law. And thirdly, he was deeply anti-Semitic. There was a connection between these flawed perceptions. Jean-Claude was of the opinion that all Jews were rich, part of an international conspiracy and deserving, therefore, of whatever hideous fate was in store for them. However, for some reason, hidden forces protected them; they were inviolate before the despised Law. He seemed to regard it as his duty to abuse the Jews on behalf of French society in general and, in particular, for all that was grievous and unfair in his own life. To avoid confronting him and coming to blows with him, I had skirted round these topics too long. Now I saw the full implications of the concessions I had made, and how compromised I had become. I had been bred to regard the Jews as a people of the Book, who had suffered for their devotion to one God. The word Jew was sacred to my family for being not the sign but the symbol of something we all deeply intuited. Jean-Claude's use of the word – the way he spat it out as if dirt clung to it – was a blasphemy that made me feel sick.

And then there was his secrecy, his concealments, his clandestine behaviour. I wondered whether he preferred the sexual experiences I imagined he must be having with all sorts of men to the one we shared. Did he live with me only

199

for the sake of appearances, perhaps? And was it defensible to live with a man because I was physically in love with him and also interested in him as an individual, if I was so suspicious of him? I never spoke of this anxious confusion with Jean-Claude. There never seemed the opportunity, and I was frightened to bring into the open subjects that were as potentially explosive as these.

Since we had been back in Reine, Jean-Claude had stopped speaking of Montaine's death as if it haunted him unduly. Indeed, the paralysis he had suffered as a result of her suicide had given way to an energetic creative vitality since he and I had been together; But he continued to insure himself against such social accidents as might reactivate his grief by avoiding the streets of Reine and its inhabitants. He must have felt his new-found vitality was precarious. He let me know every day that he longed to escape from Reine altogether. It was hardly surprising, therefore, that my refusal to accompany him to America so irked him.

'*Ma petite Opal*, I knew you'd be a *scrupulous* Hero's Muse. I knew you'd never sign the papers. You're too English. I just hoped he'd go alone.' I had told Émile I was indisposed. 'No matter!' he said, moving towards the chair in which I was sitting and unbuttoning his flies. I would make the most accomplished tart, as well as Hero's Muse, I thought, as I relieved his tension as expertly as a doctor lancing a boil.

I felt sorry for Émile. On the face of it, he was powerful: he held the lives of so many musicians – players and composers – in his grasp. But emotionally he was pitiful, held to ransom by an appalling wife. The style in which he lived in Passy was not a style to which he had always been accustomed. His were the illiterate slopes of Belleville. Nor had he wished to descend to the level of bureaucracy: he had hoped to succeed as a violinist, but lack of money (and perhaps some want of talent, to which he did not admit) had stood in his way. He married Madeleine – ten years older than himself – in gratitude for her overlooking his unpromising start. However, she never forgave him for failing to fulfil her expectations later. It was therefore generous of Émile to gain satisfaction from promoting others to success in the music world. I was feeling a certain compassion for him. He had taught me (at a tender age) how, to a partner who can accept his peculiar sexual tastes and low libido uncritically, a man may communicate his other most intimate secrets exhaustively. Émile was, in many ways, more frank with me than Jean-Claude.

I told Émile that I was thinking of leaving Jean-Claude. By saying so, I started to face this as a probable decision.

My problem was how and when to leave. Having heard myself announce my intention, I felt a peculiar sense of liberation. Returning to Reine that afternoon, I caught sight of Jean-Claude slipping into the dark urban cleft that was the rue de Sèvres, and I noticed that I felt nothing, neither curiosity nor apprehension. I had ceased to care. I had found a harsh indifference.

There are those who annihilate with violence – who devour. There are others who prefer to lay waste with words. Jean-Claude, stingy with moderation, was one such. 'Things haven't worked out as I had hoped,' he started.

Since I was not going to discuss the future with him, I did not ask him to elaborate, but I registered his disappointment and thought that, if that was how he felt, he was making it easier for me to leave him. I was too young to have become any sort of model of endurance. Nor was I waiting for rescue from above. I had taken the decision to leave him. But this did not mean I was happy with it, or knew, precisely, when and how I could carry it out. My feelings and my thoughts were engaged in a battle royal inside me. And outside there was Reine.

I was surprised to discover, now that I was going to leave it, just how attached I was to the undistinguished piecrust that was Reine, a place neither exciting nor dulling. It satisfied me, in the way that habits satisfy. Indeed, I felt a little frightened of the prospect of being torn from there, torn like ivy from a solid wall that had borne me through more than three years of my short life.

It was this image that accompanied me as I walked down the rue de Fleuve, stopping for a final *coup d'oeil* at the squat church crouching on its gravel ground. I glanced over the wall of the churchyard opposite. I did not enter. I kept on down to the river and stood for a while to watch the coal-barges slide along the black, shiny water. The market was packing up. The man who came to tie himself in chains, slip into a sack and magically – with much heaving and groaning – set himself free, had attracted the usual audience of young children. I waved to Didier and walked on between the pollarded limes. I was relieved that Didier did not run after me. I needed to be alone. I cut through the alley at the end of the Cours and wandered into the Café du Coin, the crucible of Reine les Falaises and once a place well known to Montaine. The one other place – the first being the cemetery – that Jean-Claude would never set foot in. I sat at a table in the window and drank a *filtre*. I watched as the sky curdled and darkened and the rain pelted the road with silvery stones. And while I watched, I remembered. I remembered that when I had first come to live with Jean-Claude, I had learnt to hear him thinking, and how I had not lost this gift but came to enjoy the sound of his inner voice much less. We stood too close for lies. I could not deny what I heard with my inner ear. It was not with my reason that I had fallen in love with him and come to live with him, but it was with my reason that I was going to leave him. Reason, and a sense of what is right. I was too young to exercise my intellectual force to demolish prejudices that made me sick. I did not have the skill to formulate sound arguments to counteract his taste for lawlessness, and explain why I could not partake in it. I was sick of concealments – those retentions of his. Why did he persist in trying to delude me? I satisfied myself with the knowledge that I would suffer far more from leaving him than he would suffer from my absence. Had he not said on more than one occasion, his voice weary with self-righteousness, 'I ask so little from you Opal . . .' And if that was the case, would he not find a replacement for me quite easily?

I rang Helmut's office. He was away and would not be back for two weeks. Suddenly, two weeks seemed an eternity. How on earth was I going to get through those two weeks? Only later did I wonder why it had been so important to tell Helmut I was returning to London. When eventually I got hold of him, I told him to stop making payments into my French bank account. Yes, I was leaving Paris. I was returning to London.

'Not to me, I hope.'

'No, not to you.'

'Well, as long as that's quite clear.'

I was emotionally devastated, but I was not going back with the intention of finding a man to take care of me, to pay my bills, to embellish me and play papa as Helmut had.

I was irritated that he could imagine I would want to go back to him. Three years and some months since leaving him, I had satisfied myself that, in picking me as a wife, he had done no more than is required to select a fruit from a dish with the prospect of some fleeting juiciness, but no lasting nourishment.

'Olga will try and find a room somewhere for you.'

I noticed I was grateful for this. At the back of my mind I must have hoped that if I telephoned him in advance, Helmut would help in this way. I was accustomed to his practical side.

Olga took a room for me just a mile north of Park Terrace – but in another world, the world of rooming houses. I had never known that world and I wondered how Olga felt, consigning me to it while she luxuriated in the house. For Olga had moved into Park Terrace. She had my father's money, too – more by accident than by design. I am giving poor Father the benefit of the doubt.

It had to be thus. I had money only for something just short of a slum. Helmut told me that he would continue paying my allowance until I got a job. 'In addition I'll give you whatever it costs to equip you with a suitable outfit to attend interviews. You'll have to find a job, you know.'

Of course I would. But being unqualified for anything more taxing than preparing meals and cleaning rooms, it seemed I might have no alternative but to go into service. This was a prospect that made me feel ill. It was not the work I shrank from, it was the incarceration, the lack of freedom . . .

But Helmut had another idea in mind for me: 'Apply in writing – good paper, neat handwriting – to Harrods and Fortnum's. See if they have an opening in, say, the china department – or the toys. These stores like to employ impoverished gentlewomen as sales assistants.'

I had been a dutiful daughter, an elegant accessory, a nurse and business manager in the service of three men. Now I was to be a sales assistant. Very rich men and women were going to come and patronize me: insult me. There was to be more submission. What a waste of life! But then, I was barren. I had to remember that. There was no need in the world for women like me – except to serve.

Our affair never ran its course. We were still what others term 'in love' when I left. That is to say, we still desired one another. The difference was that, whereas I sought fulfilment with Jean-Claude, he sought only to renew his desire with me. That was his problem.

I remember nothing of the days before I left Jean-Claude. Nothing at all of what we did or said; that is, until the morning of my departure.

'Shall we try again? Shall we try much harder?' I asked. I may have begged.

He did not look up from his papers. '*A quoi bon?*' he asked. What is the point?

And I knew I had been a child when I first came to live with him. I had acted foolishly.

There was no point. The vows we had made in the heat of our desire we had not kept. (How prodigal is desire!) The initial tenderness with which Jean-Claude had wooed me, had enveloped me and won me, had never developed into compassion. I was not up to sharing life with a man preoccupied, behind whose dead eyes I could detect hope stillborn. For him, the only country worth visiting was the past. His whole being had been consumed by a passionate longing to return. Fulfilment of his dream was not only physically impossible but, emotionally speaking, potentially destructive – for a dream achieved turns to dust. I was not Montaine. Childhood was a far cry away. Jean-Claude's attempt to re-create his past in music was sentenced to death like all else in his life.

I left knowing that we could not make anything together. I imagined he was destined to continue his exile with his memories in the attic at Reine. Whereas Montaine had died for her inadequacies, Jean-Claude was destined to persist because of his. I learnt from Otto before I left that Ahmed had been taken into custody prior to being deported. He did not tell me for what crime, and I did not raise the subject with Jean-Claude. I went to take my leave of Mme Guérigny. It was the first and only time I walked over to the *pavillon*, knocked on the door and entered alone.

She nodded sagely when I told her of my decision. 'I think it's for the best,' she said. She added, by way of conversation, that she must wait patiently to be relieved of the burden of living.

I walked out of the house in the rue Victorie at that uncertain time of day, hovering between work and leisure, when darkness is falling on the one but the street lights are not illuminating the other. I never went back. I never inquired after Jean-Claude and I never heard from him. From time to time, during the first few months of our separation, Otto used to ring me. But we had an understanding that no word about Jean-Claude was to be mentioned. I think it was this that made him stop telephoning me. He always liked to tell me things about my lover that my lover kept from me.

'Geza, my friend, can you see now, after all this time, why it was I could never speak about Jean-Claude when I was young and we were lovers? I was ashamed of what I had let myself in for with Jean-Claude. But, equally, I was ashamed not to have made my own way when I came back to London. Come, let us put an end to all this looking back. There is a nice little restaurant just at the corner of this street. I shall fetch my coat. I feel a heavy burden has been lifted from me. I admit, you and I did rather live our years together in the shadow of Jean-Claude, as I had lived in the shadow of Montaine. Can you adjust your memory of our time together, now that you know all that there is to know? We both need that peace, now that our days are numbered.'